PRISONER OF

Professor Raeder was in a didactic mood. He confronted his small group of paranormals as if they were students in tutorial.

'As I see it,' he said, 'the situation is of classic simplicity. It is a case of Mahomet and the mountain. We, collectively, are Mahomet, Vanessa Smith is the mountain. We must call her to come to us. We must use every means — persuasion, hypnotic suggestion, terror. We must build in her a compulsion to come to the Scottish Highlands. But, if that fails, we must be prepared to go to her. She is the burning-glass we need. She is the one who can accept your transmissions and focus them into a tight beam. She is the one who will enable your combined talents to destroy this creature Humboldt. From now on, you will conduct an assault on Vanessa round the clock.'

Prisoner of Fire

Edmund Cooper

CORONET BOOKS
Hodder and Stoughton

Copyright © 1974 by Edmund Cooper

First published in Great Britain 1974
by Hodder and Stoughton Limited

Coronet Edition 1977

Printed in Great Britain for
Hodder & Stoughton Paperbacks,
a division of Hodder & Stoughton Ltd.,
Mill Road, Dunton Green, Sevenoaks, Kent
by Richard Clay (The Chaucer Press), Ltd.,
Bungay, Suffolk

ISBN 0 340 21242 X

1

IT WAS A late spring afternoon. Vanessa was free — if
the term could be used appropriately — until roll call
and the evening meal at 18.00 At 19.00 there would be
a group session with half a dozen other paranormals
and Dr. Lindemann or Dr. Dumbarton, or both. At
20.00 she and most of the other paranormal children
would be allowed a couple of hours of censored tri-di,
or chess, or table tennis, or card games. After that bed,
the end of another day.

Vanessa sighed. Life at Random Hill Residential
School was dreadfully, boringly predictable. Dangerous
thought (low key). Somebody might be listening (also
low key). Vanessa suddenly changed gear and gave
high-key thinking to the lovely words of *The Golden
Journey to Samarkand*. That left her low-key thoughts
private. It was a form of intellectual schizophrenia to
which she had disciplined herself over the last few years.

Low key, for the hundredth time, she contemplated
the prospects of escape. She had sufficient discipline to
keep the transmission areas going strong on the poetry
of James Elroy Flecker, which, at least, gave her enough
privacy to contemplate her situation.

Random Hill was an institution, according to the
staff, where there was greater freedom for gifted
children than at any other similar school in the country.

Why, then, the electrified fences beyond the high thorn hedges that contained its one hundred acres? Why the perimeter guards and the tracker dogs? Why the infinite variations on *mañana* if anyone expressed a desire to see the outside world?

I am seventeen years old, thought Vanessa (low key). I have been a prisoner here for more than ten years. I must get out, even if the world is as dangerous as they say. I must get out.

But where were the paranormal powers that would enable one to pass through an electrified fence?

Vanessa was sitting on a grassy knoll under a huge oak tree, barely two hundred yards from the large nineteen-century house that had been converted into a school for paranormals. She was in full view of the staff wing, and had deliberately chosen her spot for that very reason, reasoning that if she remained visible, people would probably be less curious about what she was thinking. Sometimes it worked that way, sometimes it didn't. But if you hid yourself away or appeared secretive, there was a very strong chance that they would use a rapport or a seeker to find out what you were thinking and where you were.

You could never feel a rapport, though you could feel a seeker. She had always interpreted the probe of a seeker as a mental sensation analogous to a very gentle hand stroking her hair. The moment she experienced such a sensation, she knew that her thoughts were no longer private.

Vanessa lay back on the grass, stretching herself luxuriously. She got tired of the Samarkand block and switched to music — a simple folk tune: Greensleeves. Somebody had once told her that it had been composed by an ancient king of England.

With Greensleeves dominating the high-key area,

6

Vanessa allowed her low-key thoughts to roam. Really, she told herself, she was in danger of becoming paranoid. There was no one at Random Hill of whom she need be afraid. She had the best extra-sensory rating of all forty-three chidren. The next esrate was Dugal Nemo, and he was only nine years old. Also he was Vanessa's friend. The trouble with Dugal was that he was a trusting boy, easily led; and he was a first-class seeker as well as a developing rapport. But surely there could be nothing to fear from Dugal?

Both she and Dugal were orphans, knowing nothing at all of their parents. It was a bond. Even if they had not had high esrates, they would still have felt like brother and sister.

Vanessa dismissed her fears of surveillance and concentrated on the problem of escape.

Dugal tried to make himself comfortable in the chair that was far too big for him, and took the proffered bar of chocolate from Dr. Lindemann.

"May I eat it now?"

Dr. Lindemann laughed. "What would you do if I said no? You would clutch it in your hot little hand until it became a sticky mess. Yes, Dugal, eat the chocolate — but please don't get it all over your face, there's a good fellow."

They were in Dr. Lindemann's study. Through the window it was possible to see Vanessa lying on the grass under a big tree. Dugal liked Dr. Lindemann very much. He was the youngest of the scientists at Random Hill, and he had a sense of fun, and he laughed a lot. Also he was an inexhaustible source of chocolate bars.

"We are very pleased with you, Dugal. You are our star pupil. One day, when you are grown up, you will maintain a communications link with the solar colonies. You will be an important man."

Dugal munched his chocolate and shot a wild probe at Dr. Lindemann's mind. As expected, he hit the barrier. Funny how all these scientists had the same mind barrier. Perhaps they were deformed.

"Vanessa is better than me," said Dugal.

Dr. Lindemann shrugged. "She's much older, and she is only a girl."

"Some girls are all right," said Dugal carefully. "I mean, Vanessa doesn't have to be no good just because she is a girl."

"No. But girls are not usually as ambitious as boys, Dugal. Probably, Vanessa will marry and have children and forget all about her special gifts."

"I want to be the best 'path in the world," said Dugal, munching. "I want to be able to talk to people out among the stars."

"And you might be," said Dr. Lindemann. "You know people like me are blind, Dugal. But even we blind scientists know a great deal about paranormal powers. If you follow our teaching, you might well become the best telepath in the world . . . You like Vanessa a lot, don't you?"

"She's the greatest — for a girl, I mean."

Dr. Lindemann laughed. "I bet you can't probe her."

Dugal looked surprised. "Of course I can, Dr. Lindemann. You know that. Ask her to open, and I'll probe all you want."

"What I mean," said Dr. Lindemann silkily, "is that I don't think you can probe her if we don't ask her to open."

Dugal finished his chocolate, licked his fingers. "I could, too. But — but would it be right?"

"She is your friend, isn't she?"

8

"Yes."

"Then, of course it would be all right."

"You are sure?"

"Yes, I'm sure . . . Try it, Dugal. Tell me what she is thinking."

Dugal closed his eyes. "When the great markets by the sea shut fast," he said. "All that calm Sunday that goes on and on. When even lovers find their peace at last. And earth is but a star that once had shone." He opened his eyes. "That is what she is thinking, Dr. Lindemann. It doesn't make much sense, does it? But that is what she is thinking."

"Poetry," said Dr. Lindemann. "That is what it is. Vanessa is amusing herself." He gazed at her through the window. She did not seem to have moved. "Do you think Vanessa felt your probe, Dugal?"

"I don't know. I don't think so. I was very gentle. Can I go now, Dr. Lindemann?"

The scientist smiled. "Soon. Soon. You want to be rushing about in the sunshine, no doubt. Very right and proper. Children should be like healthy young animals . . Do you like Random Hill, Dugal?"

"Yes, sir. Very much."

"You are happy with us here?"

"Yes, sir. Everybody is very kind."

"Good. Good . . . Just for fun, Dugal, try to probe Vanessa again. Let us see if she is still enjoying her poetry."

Obediently, Dugal closed his eyes once more. "It's music," he said after a moment or two. "Nice music. Shall I whistle the tune?"

"No. There's no need. Vanessa seems to be in a happy mood . . . I wonder if she is thinking of anything else but the music? Sometimes people make little

9

tunes for themselves while one part is busy with other thoughts. Can you probe deeper, Dugal?"

Dugal looked anxious. "Vanessa might not like it."

Dr. Lindemann shrugged. Miraculously another chocolate bar had appeared in his hand. "It's only an experiment, Dugal. We make experiments like this all day long, don't we?"

Dugal was hesitant. "Shall I run out and ask her, Dr. Lindemann? Ask her if I can try a deep probe, I mean?"

Lindemann pretended to stifle a yawn. "It is not that important, Dugal." He handed over the chocolate bar. "Besides, we could make secrecy part of the experiment, couldn't we? But if you don't think you are good enough to make a deep probe in secret . . ."

"Oh, I can do it," said Dugal with all the confidence of a child.

"Well, then, let us make our secret experiment. And after that you can go and run off all the energy you have absorbed from two bars of chocolate." Dr. Lindemann laughed. "But if you get spots and have to see Matron, I shall deny having given you any chocolate at all."

Dugal grinned conspiratorily. Then he closed his eyes. "The same nice music. Very loud. I'm going underneath it, but she feels me. She knows someone is there . . . The music is louder, her thoughts — her thoughts are scrambling away . . . There is something about electricity. That is all I can get. The music is now very loud." Dugal opened his eyes. He looked troubled.

"Electricity," said Dr. Lindemann. "Music and electricity. How interesting. You did very well, Dugal."

"Can I go now?"

"Yes, you can go, Dugal. Remember it was a secret

10

experiment. I can assure you Vanessa won't mind."

"Yes, sir." Dugal left the room feeling vaguely unhappy.

Vanessa shivered. Twice she thought she had felt the wind in her hair. But when the deep probe came, she knew it had not been the wind. Only one person could pass her blocks — if he wanted to. But why would Dugal do it? Not for his own childish curiosity. He was too gentle, too sensitive for that. Someone had conned him. Lindemann, Dumbarton, Professor Holroyd — somebody.

Did it matter who? They were all the enemy, all jailers. All that mattered was what Dugal had found and what he had told. While she was contemplating the situation, Vanessa used what she considered to be her strongest block — an old nonsense song with a monotonous refrain: Ten Green Bottles. Once she started that compulsive sequence running through her head, she could be reasonably sure that even Dugal would be blocked by the idiotic repetition.

The important thing was not to let anyone know that she had noticed the probe. The important thing was just to lie back on the grass and appear to enjoy the blue sky, the spring sunlight.

Vanessa had closed her eyes, and did not seem to be aware of Dr. Lindemann's presence until he spoke to her.

"Are you asleep, Vanessa?" he said softly.

She opened her eyes, squinted up at him against the sky. He was not bad-looking for a middle-aged man of forty, or thereabouts. She knew that, apart from his professional concern, he found her sexually interesting also.

"Not asleep, Dr. Lindemann. Just daydreaming."

"Oh. About anything special?"

So he was the one who had used Dugal. She had an inspiration. Carry the war to the enemy. "Nothing important. I was just thinking about the electrified fences."

Dr. Lindemann appeared to stroke a beard that did not exist. "Interesting. Do you know why you were thinking about the electrified fences."

She sat up. "Yes. It seems so sad — especially on a spring day — that we are shut off from the rest of the world, and it is shut off from us."

Dr. Lindemann smiled. "Precautions, Vanessa. Nothing but precautions. You lead a sheltered existence. You are lucky. The outside world could be a very dangerous place to people such as you. You watch tri-di. You know the level of violence that exists in our so-called civilised society. The masses are always looking for scapegoats — communists, catholics, immigrants, anarchists, spies. Even espeople like you. Have you considered that you are fortunate in being so well protected?"

"Yes. And I am thankful that I have a secure life with good friends and good teachers. But, just occasionally, I feel like a prisoner."

Dr. Lindemann laughed. "A morbid thought. You are not a prisoner, Vanessa. You are a privileged person. Soon you will be eighteen. For a few months you are still a minor, and your welfare is our responsibility. But when you attain your majority, if you still want to leave, we shall not stand in your way. If you still want to leave, you will be able to walk out through the gate with nearly a thousand Euros in your pocket and no obligations to Random Hill whatsoever."

Vanessa remembered (low key) the last person who had done just that. James Grey, a boy who was the

12

best telepath that Random Hill had ever developed. It was nearly a year ago.

Vanessa and James had been psychologically intimate. By mutual consent they had agreed not to use blocks with each other. James had been convinced that the Random Hill set-up was a complicated conspiracy to restrict the liberty of paranormals. On his eighteenth birthday, he had decided to leave the institution and try his luck in the outside world. He had been given money, his identity card and the clothes he needed. Within an hour of leaving Random Hill, he had been found dead — horribly murdered.

His body had been brought back, and the older children had been allowed to see it, if they wished. Some of them did so wish, Vanessa among them. The wounds had been skilfully concealed, but not too skilfully. Especially for young people with some imagination.

Vanessa recalled his last, anguished transmission. "Don't try it. Not this way. They have thugs waiting..."

So she said to Dr. Lindemann: "I don't suppose I shall ever want to leave Random Hill or reject the training I have been given. I have too many friends here. Where would I find such friends outside?"

"Perhaps you are right. But don't let me influence you, my dear. Make up your own mind. There is plenty of time."

"Yes," said Vanessa. "There is plenty of time."

Though she knew that time was running out. How long could you live in a situation where you had to use mental blocks to maintain your privacy and be yourself?

2

IN THE SUMMER of 1973, Jenny Smith, aged eighteen, daughter of a Sussex farmer, had run away from home. Jenny had been an exceptionally intelligent child and had distinguished herself at school. Her teachers had discovered a peculiarity. In any form of oral examination, where the teacher already knew the answers to the questions being asked, Jenny invariably gained one hundred per cent. In any oral examination where the teacher did not know the answers to the questions, she still scored outstandingly high marks, but never one hundred per cent. In written examinations, whether the presiding teacher knew the answers or not, Jenny still scored one hundred per cent or very near to it.

Her teachers wanted her to go on to university. So did Jenny. Her father, a kindly but stolid man of fifty-three, did not. Having recently buried his wife, he saw no reason why he should continue to pay good wages to a housekeeper when Jenny was old enough to take over.

Jenny had wanted to take a degree in English Literature. Her father vetoed the notion. Jenny became an unpaid housekeeper on an isolated downland farm that was ten miles from the nearest town. She stood the isolation — physical, emotional, intellectual — through one long winter. Then she ran away.

She took ten pounds out of the housekeeping money, packed her few clothes in a battered hold-all, walked five miles to the main road and thumbed a lift to London.

She went to an employment agency and got a temporary job. Since she could not type or take shorthand, it was a very lowly job. She became a filing clerk for a company in the City which specialised in the marketing of petrochemical products.

She found herself a room in Bayswater, and was content for a while to cook meals over a single gas ring, to listen to the radio and to read the books it was necessary to read if one hoped to take an external degree in English Literature.

After a time, she was promoted to the grandiose status of Information Assistant, which meant that she had to answer the phone and search for the data required by high-powered executives. Sometimes, they wished to know about the seismic surveys in Brazil, or natural gas deposits in Australia, or butyl rubber production in the U.S.A., or crude oil reserves in the U.S.S.R. She was rather good on these kind of problems, particularly if she had to consult a specialist. She seemed to know the answers almost before they were given.

Meanwhile, she met John. John had a room in the same apartment house. He had at the time a good job supervising girls who packed chocolate bars in a large factory. He was a Rhodesian; and his complexion was dark enough, his cheekbones broad enough, his hair black enough to suggest a touch of negro blood somewhere along the line.

John was a drop-out arts graduate, an idealist. He could have taken some sinecure in a museum of fine arts or a commercial gallery, or even in the expanding sub-industry of post-graduate research. Instead, he chose to drift. The job in the chocolate factory was, so he said, simply the means by which he could buy an air-ticket to Japan. He said he wanted to take a look at Japanese culture and also find out what the radical students were doing.

John and Jenny were never in love; but each had an uncanny ability to know what the other was thinking and feeling. Sometimes, they seemed to indulge in conversations where neither opened their lips. Eventually, they went to bed together — as much for mutual comfort and an extension of intimacy as for sexual desire.

Within six weeks of their getting to know each other, John was killed — stupidly and absurdly — in a demonstration outside the American Embassy in Grosvenor Square. The demonstration had started peacefully enough as a disciplined protest against the alleged charges of malpractice against an American negro doctor in Alabama. But a lot of people turned up — it being a fine day — the provos became violent, and the mounted police, that splendid British anachronism, were called in. Somebody threw a nails-and-gelignite bomb, intended for the mounted police. It fell short. Two demonstrators were killed and seven injured. John was one of the dead.

By that time, though she did not yet know it, Jenny was pregnant. Somehow, she learned to accept his death. Somehow she managed to hold down her job in the city. Indeed, she prospered. She learned much about the company for which she worked, and she learned something of the manipulation of stocks and shares. She learned not so much from what people said as from what they thought.

While the baby swelled in her stomach, she learned

16

to make money. By the time the child was born, she had become intent upon making money as a means to power.

Also she had met a bright young man — not empathetic in the way that John had been empathetic — but sensitive enough and attractive enough to draw her allegiance and physical desire. He wanted to marry her, but he did not want to be encumbered with a child not his.

Jenny bore her baby and put it into a home. Then she married her bright young man and became very, very rich. She never went back to the farm in Sussex, and she never enquired after the welfare of her daughter. When she was thirty-nine years old, she took an overdose of sleeping tablets. But by then she knew what had happened to Vanessa.

3

IT WAS SHORTLY after midnight. Vanessa had left the dormitory and had stolen a pole from the gymnasium and also a four-pound lumber axe from the forester's hut. Tonight she would be free or dead.

She had been practising pole-jumping for several days. She hoped it had not been noticed, but she did not count on it. In practice jumps she had managed to leap nearly ten feet. The electrified fence was eight feet high. Theoretically, she should have easy clearance. But before she could get to the fence, there was the thorn hedge. A narrow avenue would have to be cut through it. She needed at least twenty paces for her run.

Vanessa wore only the dark blue trousers and vest and the light plimsolls she used for physical education. They were the only things she could think of that were practical enough for the task ahead. Fortunately, it was a warm night. Fortunately, also, there was some moonlight.

The moon was both friend and enemy. She needed its light to hack a way through the thorn hedge, to see where the fence was and where to plant the pole when she made her leap. But it exposed her. It made her feel naked.

This was not the first time Vanessa had been out

late at night. She had used several evenings to check when the guards and the dogs made their rounds. They were very regular. They came round at half-hourly intervals until midnight, then at one-hourly intervals until dawn. The midnight rounds had just been made.

Vanessa had chosen to make her leap over that part of the fence that was farthest away from the school. It was nearly a quarter of a mile from the main buildings; and it had the additional advantage of being partially screened from the school by a group of beech trees.

Cutting a way through the hedge was going to be noisy — and she would have to skip very carefully over the thorn stumps — but these were risks that could not be avoided. Better to face them than remain a prisoner or, in desperation, leave as poor James had left.

Exposing herself as little as possible as she crossed the moonlit lawns, Vanessa had darted from the shadow to patch of shadow, like a true creature of the night. Constantly, she looked back apprehensively over her shoulder. Constantly she ran through a verbal mind-block to defeat any accidental or deliberate probe. Dugal would be asleep; and without Dugal the parapsychologists of Random Hill were almost blind.

She arrived at the place she had chosen, laid down the axe and pole, and leaned against a beech tree for a while to get her breath and renew her courage. She looked around her. The world was curiously still and beautiful. How easy it would be to take back the pole and the axe, creep back into the dormitory and accept the security of clean sheets, regular meals, an orderly existence.

But the price you had to pay for such security was too high. You had to surrender freedom of action.

That could be borne. What could not be borne was that you also had to surrender freedom of thought. Vanessa, though only seventeen, knew very well what the parapsychologists of Random Hill were doing. They were intent upon turning a group of gifted children into controlled sensing machines. The government needed people with paranormal powers for sophisticated techniques of communication, for plain simple espionage, for non-verbal interrogation, for internal security and for every dirty game that governments throughout the world were prepared to play to maintain their own authority. From odd remarks that Dr. Lindemann had made, Vanessa knew that China, Russia, America and most of the other countries that presumed to play at international politics were rapidly developing their own paranormal resources.

Vanessa did not want to be part of any political game, dirty or clean. She simply wanted to be herself, her own woman. She wanted to live in peace. It was a simple ambition and, in the world of 1990, a brave ambition. There was a price tag on that, also.

She took a last look round at the peaceful, nocturnal world. How clean everything seemed. How clean and clear. She looked up at the stars. Many were obscured by the haze of moonlight; but enough burned to indicate that truly the universe was too poignantly beautiful for people to allow themselves to be destroyed in meaningless ways.

She brushed tears from her face, lifted the axe and approached the thorn hedge. She had been able to practise pole-jumping. She had not been able to practise cutting down thorn hedges. She had no idea how long it would take or how much noise she would make.

This was the testing time.

An owl hooted.

Vanessa chose her spot and swung the axe. She aimed low, where the tough wood entered the ground. The first blow glanced off, the axe-head was buried in earth. Vanessa pulled it clear and swung again. This time the axe bit. Not deeply, but it bit. The hedge shook. Overhanging thorns snagged at her hair, scratched her face, hooked in her vest. Vanessa ignored them and swung again with all her might. The blow sounded like a pistol shot through the still, clear night. She ignored the blood on her face, the scratches on her body, wrenched the axe loose and swung again. And again. And again.

After perhaps ten blows, there was a creaking noise. Then a section of the hedge fell forward, almost upon her. Oblivious of the sharp thorns, she tried to drag it clear, but it was still attached to the stump by a few annoying strands of wood.

She swung the axe once more with all the strength of frenzy and despair. She could hear dogs barking in the distance. In a few minutes, perhaps even in a few seconds, the guards would come. The last axe blow severed the remaining strands, and she was able to drag the clump of thorn hedge clear of the gap.

Now she had a clear run, provided she remembered to skip over the stump. She dropped the axe and found her vaulting pole. She could not grip it properly. Her hands were sticky with sweat and blood.

But it was now or never. She could see the dogs, and she could see the guards running after them, electric torches swinging from side to side.

Suddenly an icy coldness came over her. It was as if all emotion were banished, as if she had become physically detached from her body. Calmly she went close to the fence, turned and paced her running distance from it. Then she turned once more, the pole held in both hands, testing its weight and attitude. The dogs and the guards were little more than a hundred yards away now. They would be upon her in seconds.

She gazed at the moonlight, shining upon the formidable barbed wires of the electrified fence.

"I can only die once," she told herself coolly, as if it were a kind of consolation.

Even as she poised to start her run, she heard a woman's voice in her head. It was not a voice she knew, but yet it seemed familiar. "Don't do it! Don't do it! Don't do it!"

"I will do it!" shouted Vanessa aloud.

With practised grace, she started the run, taking long powerful strides, remembering to skip over the thorn stump in the gap in the hedge without disturbing her essential rhythm. Then all coherent thought was lost. Her body became a finely tuned machine.

She gathered speed, the fence loomed before her, she thrust the point of the pole down into yielding earth, and leaped. The pole bent under the impetus of her forward movement, responded to the lift, jerked back into its natural straight shape, and hurled her over the fence.

As she let go she was aware of sparks and crackling noises. Then she was falling on to soft earth. She picked herself up, turned and saw the guards and their dogs, impotent on the other side of the fence. It would take them a long time to reach the main gate; but perhaps they could radio for help. Vanessa turned and ran. There was only one direction in which to run, and that was away. She ran until she thought her lungs would burst. It was several hours until daylight. That was when the search would begin in earnest. During the

22

remaining hours of darkness, she must put as much distance between herself and Random Hill as possible.

In a luxurious penthouse flat at the top of an expensive block in London West One, Jenny Pargetter, née Jenny Smith, woke up screaming.

"Don't do it! Don't do it! Don't do it! "

Simon, her husband, switched on the light and tried to comfort her.

"What is it, love? A nightmare?"

She was shivering and shaking. "Yes, a nightmare."

Simon kissed her, held her close, attempting to dismiss it. "Not to worry, love. Too much lobster thermidor. Maybe too many pink gins. Serves me right for embroiling you with ghastly stockbrokers. Won't do it again."

Jenny tried to respond to his caresses and could not. "It was so real, Simon. So vividly real."

"Tell me about it."

She passed a hand over her forehead, gripped her temples tightly. "Well, I seemed to be a young girl, in some kind of institution, trying to break out. There was an electrified fence, and I was terrified of it because I knew I would have to pole-vault it."

Simon got out of bed, put on his silk dressing-gown, went out of the bedroom and returned with a bottle of brandy and two glasses.

"One for you?"

"No, thank you, darling. As you say, too many pink gins."

"It wasn't an accusation."

"I know it wasn't."

Simon poured himself a large brandy. "A young girl, you say?"

"Yes."

23

"Can you remember anything else?"

"Not much. There were dogs and men in uniform. It was frightening."

"Did you — or she — make the jump?"

"Yes."

"Did you — or she — survive?"

"I — I think so."

Simon took a deep draught of the brandy. 'Hell,' he thought. 'Vandalism. One should sip this stuff and savour it.'

"A young girl," said Simon. "How young?"

"Sixteen, seventeen, eighteen — I don't know."

"Vanessa?"

Jenny gave a shrill laugh. "You read too much into nightmares."

"Vanessa?"

"It could be — I suppose."

Simon poured himself more brandy. "Darling, you underestimated me. I would not have resented her. At least, I don't think I would ... I'll make enquiries tomorrow. O.K.?"

"O.K."

"Well, then. Have a brandy and snuggle close. No more nightmares, I promise."

4

VANESSA RAN UNTIL she could not even feel the ache in her rubbery legs any more, and only knew that she was still alive because the aching pain in her chest would not go away and because she seemed to have to muster a gigantic effort of will to draw in each sobbing breath to power the worn-out, overworked engine of her body.

She ran like a mindless automaton, through woods, across ditches and ploughed fields, through a small stream whose icy water had refreshed her temporarily. At first, she had heard the dogs behind her; and the sound of their eager barking had supercharged the adrenalin pumped into her bloodstream. For a while her feet seemed to have barely touched the ground. Presently, the sound of the dogs was left far behind. They could travel as fast as she could, faster. They were more efficient, more tireless; but they were held back by the men. The guards were stronger than Vanessa; but they lacked her will. For them the chase was not a matter of life and death. For her it was. And so she outdistanced them easily in the first hour of pursuit.

As she ran, a mindless song repeated itself endlessly in her head; Ten green bottles hanging on a wall ... It went on and on; and as soon as the last green bottle had fallen there was a new wall with ten more green bottles to take its place.

Instinctively, she travelled south. She crossed two main roads and a motorway, almost oblivious of the blinding lights, the blaring horns. She climbed fences and fell across ditches. She ran on through the night until the stars winked out one by one and the moon danced crazily like a yellow balloon in the wind. She ran herself into the ground, and lay where she had fallen, unconscious, spent. She did not know it, but another fifty paces would have taken her to a barn where there was plenty of hay to make a soft, warm bed.

She just lay where she had fallen in a field of winter wheat. She lay on her face while tiny spiders crawled over her unconscious body and while dew formed on her hair.

She returned to consciousness shortly after daybreak. She awoke because her body was one great, terrifying ache. She tried to stand up, and cried out aloud with pain. Slowly, pitifully, she compelled her limbs to obey her. She forgot all about mental blocks. Let who would probe her mind. All they would discover would be agony. Rather than preserve secrecy, it was more important that she concentrated on making her limbs obey her, that she concentrated on finding food and something to drink.

Luck was with her. There were free-range hens on the farm. One had made a nest in the wheat field and had laid eggs there in the sublime belief that she would be allowed to rear a clutch of chicks. Vanessa saw the nest and started cracking eggs. Fortunately, the hen had never been allowed to run with a cock. The eggs were infertile. Vanessa sat cross-legged, cracking the eggs and swallowing their contents greedily while the hen strutted about, raised her neck feathers and swore mightily. Vanessa tried to make soothing noises; but the hen was not impressed.

In the same field she found an old stone drinking trough, doubtless belonging to the long-dead days when farmers once used horses to draw ploughs. The trough was encrusted with moss and lichen; but there was still some water — probably rainwater from recent showers — in it.

Vanessa cupped her hands and drank greedily. The water tasted faintly brackish but it also tasted good. With the raw eggs, it seemed to pour life and energy into her resilient body. As she was finishing drinking, she heard a voice. Glancing over her shoulder, she saw a man near the barn. He was beckoning her.

She panicked. The receding pain in her limbs forgotten, she began to run once more. Across the field, over a five-barred gate. South ... South ...

The sun had risen above the horizon. She began to hear voices in her head.

'Vanessa, come back. Come back! You won't be punished. Dr. Lindemann promises that you won't be punished.'

She recognised Dugal's pattern. Dear, simple-minded Dugal. He was transmitting what they wanted him to transmit. Doubtless the fee would be a chocolate bar.

She didn't try to say anything to Dugal. There was no point in trying to say anything. Whatever thoughts she uttered would only make him more unhappy. He would not be able to understand why she had run away; he was far too young, far too trusting, to be able to comprehend tyranny. There was no point in putting doubt into his mind, setting him in conflict with the people who controlled his destiny.

So, wearily, as she ran, she set up the insane mental

block once more: Ten Green Bottles. If they could not persuade Dugal to probe beneath it, they would try Meriona, or Thomas or Greg. Meriona was almost the same age as Vanessa and hated her. Meriona was plain, Vanessa was pretty. But, fortunately, Meriona didn't have much of an esfactor. There was little to fear from her. Nor was there much to fear from Thomas or Greg. Dugal was the only dangerous one, and he was Vanessa's friend.

Automatically, Vanessa kept away from villages. She travelled across farmland and through wooded country. Even in 1990 much of southern England remained unspoiled. Apart from the incursion of super-highways, telephone poles and the occasional phalanx of pylons, the countryside had changed little in a hundred years.

Running soon tired her, and brought the aches back. After a time she tried a routine of running one hundred strides, then walking one hundred paces. It helped; though it was hard at the end of the walking session to start running again. Frequently, because of sheer fatigue, she had to relax the mind block; and then the whispers were in her head. 'Come back! Come back!' Sometimes the transmission patterns were Dugal's, sometimes they were unrecognisable.

She kept her eyes open for people. When she saw them — chiefly farm employees — she would saunter along as if she were just taking a leisurely walk.

The sun climbed up towards its zenith. Shortly before noon, Vanessa saw a helicopter. It was not making the usual kind of straight-line journey that helicopters make from point A to point B. It was circling, weaving, hovering. It was looking.

She was in a field of young barley when she saw it coming from the north. She was not more than twenty

28

paces from the cover of a substantial patch of woodland. She ran faster than she had thought she could run, leaped a gate, fell in a heap, picked herself up and staggered into the cover of the trees.

There she fainted.

When she became conscious once more, she found that she was cold and shivering.

There were stars in the sky, and a pale watery moon. She shivered and cried. Presently, she picked herself up and tried to go on. She did not get very far.

5

DR. ROLAND BADEL had been a recluse for almost a year. He liked his solitary existence, although he noted with clinical detachment the withdrawal symptoms of the hermit. The scars on his face had healed well, and the thin white line that showed where his throat had been inefficiently cut was more or less permanently concealed by a cravat; though there were very few occasions when anyone else was likely to see it. But once a day, at least, Badel had to look at it, when he shaved. He still had the nightmares; but he no longer trembled or felt the sweat break out when he saw the scar. And that, certainly, was a good sign.

He was a trained psychologist. For nearly ten years he had worked for the National Psychological Laboratory on the development of personality-reshaping programmes. He had been head of a team that tested such programmes on anti-social persons. Or, as he himself used to put it bluntly, he had been head mechanic in a human repair shop. Chiefly, he had tested his programme on criminals, psychopaths, anarchists, subversives and sexual deviants. Upon such flotsam, he and his team had tried aversion therapy, psychoanalysis (Jungian and Freudian), twilight sleep, deprivation sequences, suspended animation, stress stimuli, lobotomy, electroplexy, controlled starvation programmes, hypnotherapy and plain brainwashing. Sometimes, some of the treatments had worked — or had appeared to work — with some of the specimens. Sometimes, nothing had worked. Sometimes, after sustained treatment, the end product was a cabbage, not a person.

The aims of the project were laudible. If you could use psychological techniques to rehabilitate anti-social persons, you could do away with prisons and a frighteningly large number of nut-houses. Capital punishment had already been discarded as a means of dealing with violence, and the conventional prison system had already proved its own inadequacy. Therefore something new had to be tried. Personality reshaping had appealed not only to the popular imagination but to the government also. It was supposed to be humane. And, anyway, if it worked it would save a great deal of the taxpayer's money.

The trouble was sometimes it worked and sometimes it didn't. And there was no certain means of predicting the result. Roland Badel had hoped that his researches would have yielded rehabilitation formulas for different psychological types. They didn't. They left him with half a face and a white line across his throat.

The disaster occurred because he had been too sure of himself, too confident in the treatment schedule he had devised for an eighteen-year-old girl named Susan Stride, who had murdered her father.

Susan was not criminally insane. She was just a girl who had endured too much stress and had finally exploded in a fit of uncontrollable violence under extreme provocation. Or so it seemed.

Her case history appeared to be a classic pattern of rejection. Her mother had died when she was fifteen. She was an only child; and thereafter she tried to keep

31

house for her father, doing all the things that her mother would have done, and doing them as efficiently as possible. Her father ran a prosperous art gallery; and their standard of living was good. After his wife's death, though he was content to let Susan run the household, he took a succession of mistresses, bringing each home for a while, until he tired of her and sent her packing. The ritual was monotonously invariable. Susan was expected to be pleasant to each woman and treat her as a potential stepmother. When the time came for departure, Susan's father always contrived to be curiously absent, leaving an adolescent girl to deal with mature rejected women, to help them dry their tears, to help them pack their belongings, and to help them leave the flat with as much dignity as possible.

One evening, Susan's father came home drunk. Blind drunk. At least, that was the way Susan told it in session, under hypnosis and under truth drug. Ergo, that was the way it was.

His mind being befuddled, he apparently thought that Susan was his latest conquest and that she was making difficulties. His only method of resolving difficulties with women was to take them to bed. He tried to make love to Susan. He was a strong man, and he was suffering from too much alcohol and too many delusions. Susan broke a gin bottle over his head without much effect. At least, that was the way she told it. And the telling was very convincing.

He knocked her half silly and dragged her to the bedroom. According to Susan. There, while he was struggling with his clothes, she found another gin bottle and smashed that also over his head. Then she went berserk and sawed through his throat with a fragment of glass.

Such was the story that could not be broken down by drugs, by hypnosis or by analysis.

Dr. Badel came to the conclusion that there really was not a great deal of complexity in Susan's case. He had found no signs of schizophrenia. She was a highly inhibited girl; and it was perfectly natural that she should be withdrawn, remote, listless, depressed after such a traumatic experience. She needed chiefly to unburden herself, to shed the load of guilt, to come to terms with the extreme provocation that had temporarily unbalanced her.

The trouble was that Susan would not respond or co-operate unless she were drugged or hypnotised. But she needed to be in full possession of her faculties to go through the integration process. A simple but crude solution might have been found in lobotomy, a temporary solution in electroplexy. But Dr. Badel did not want to use such extreme measures. The girl was young; if she could be coaxed through the crisis, she might look forward to a long and creative life.

He hit upon the oldest trick in the book to get her to respond. The rest of the staff were instructed to be deliberately hostile to Susan, to make life difficult for her, to quarrel with her, to deprive her of luxuries, to interrupt her sleep, even to tamper with her food. Only Badel would be sympathetic, ever ready to deal with real or imagined grievances. Thus he would gain her confidence.

When the time was ripe, a careful little drama was staged. One of the attractive women psychologists, who had been instructed to be especially hostile, was to be discovered by Badel physically ill-treating Susan. There would then be a scene where he would shout at the woman, dismiss her from the case and eject her bodily from Susan's room. The negative parallels that Dr.

33

Badel sought to establish were obvious. This was what Susan would have liked her father to do to the women who invaded Susan's world.

The drama went off perfectly. It worked like a charm. In the cause of science, Dr. Badel's pretty colleague allowed her face to be slapped as, struggling and protesting, she was thrust from Susan's room.

Dr. Badel promised that the hated woman would never return. After that incident, Susan began to respond, slowly. At first, during her daily sessions with Badel, she would only answer questions — chiefly yes or no answers. Later, she began to volunteer information. Eventually, she learned to talk freely about her childhood, her relations with her mother, even the traumatic sequence that led to the killing of her father.

The daily sessions of analysis took place in Dr. Badel's office. The dialogue was discreetly taped. Afterwards he reviewed each session and summarised his findings. After two weeks he confidently predicted that Susan would soon be able to take up a normal existence once more. He thought that she might find some kind of fulfilment, and expiation, working in a hospital.

One day, Susan asked if the analysis session could take place in her own room. Dr. Badel saw no reason why this should not be so. But when he came to Susan's room, he was amazed to discover that she was wearing only a shortie nightdress.

While he was registering the implications, she wedged a chair back under the door handle. Then she advanced upon him, flung her arms round his neck and said: "I love you. I love you. Please make love to me. Please. Please! I'm a woman, you know. I can give you great pleasure."

As she kissed him on the lips, he suddenly realised that he had been totally wrong. He was too late.

"Susan, I think you are a marvellous girl, but — "

"But I'm not good enough for screwing?" she demanded imperiously, standing back. The transformation from girl into tigress was too fast for Dr. Badel's reactions.

"Do you like me?" she demanded in an unnatural voice.

"Yes, but — "

"No buts. Do you love me?" Her eyes were wild.

"Yes, but not in the way you think."

"I said no buts." Her voice had hardened. "If you like me, if you love me, do with me what you do with all those other bloody women!"

He didn't even have time to voice an answer. She saw the answer in his eyes.

And she reached for the water carafe by the bed. Then she hit him with it again and again. Because she was young, and because she was demented, her movements were too fast for him.

She had hit him several times before the thick glass broke. He fell to his knees, protesting feebly, not knowing what he was saying, because the heavy carafe crashed down again and again. And Susan was screaming.

Somebody heard the noise, and eventually the door was battered down. They found Susan Stride sitting on the chest of Dr. Roland Badel, senior psychologist. She had a thick, jagged piece of glass in her hand. She had already cut one side of his face to pieces, and she was busy sawing through his throat.

Susan, having then retreated into catatonia, was sent to an asylum for the incurably insane.

While he lay in hospital, recovering from injuries that by all known laws ought to have resulted in death,

Dr. Roland Badel knew that he had stopped playing God for ever.

He should have realised that Susan Stride had killed her father not because he assaulted her but because he rejected her. He should have been able to diagnose schizophrenia. He should have prescribed depth sedation at least while he thought it all out. He should have been *competent*.

So now here he was, having himself withdrawn from society, living the life of a recluse in an isolated country cottage with the knowledge that a great part of his life had been wasted.

Personality-reshaping programmes! He could not even reshape his own personality enough to enable him to make social contacts, to move in the world of people.

He kept chickens, grew his own vegetables, cooked for himself. He did not have tri-di or even a V-phone. Sometimes he read novels — nineteenth-century novels: Dickens, Thackeray, Jane Austen, the Brontës. Sometimes he listened to music: Tschaikowsky, Beethoven, Chopin, Grieg, Liszt. He drank a great deal and went for long walks in the woods. He tried to abolish the twentieth century, along with the recollections of a failed psychologist. Some nights, he woke up screaming.

One morning, after a bad night, he got up early and went out to feed the chickens. It was a damp morning with mist on the hills and a fine drizzle drifting down to earth.

In the chicken run, he found a girl lying on her face, filthy, wet, unconscious. In one of her hands were the crushed remains of two eggs. A hungry chicken was pecking at one of her ears, and had caused blood to come.

The girl was wearing a dark blue vest and dark blue

trousers. She was pitifully thin. The drizzle had left a fine lacing of jewels in her hair. Surprised and shaken, Roland Badel turned her over and looked at her face. For a few terrible moments, he had to stop himself from shouting and running. She seemed to look just like Susan Stride. Then, when he had calmed down, he saw that she was quite different. About the same age, but different.

Under the mud her face was dreadfully pale, but she was still breathing. He managed to lift her up and carry her into the cottage. He put her on a battered settee, found a blanket and laid it over her, and lighted a wood fire. Then he poured himself a very large whisky, drank it and poured another.

Then he sat on a chair, staring at her, trying to think what to do.

6

VANESSA OPENED HER eyes. She had not the strength to
lift herself up, but she could move her head a little. It
took her some time to focus. She saw a fire, a bright,
comfortable wood fire, and gazed at it gratefully for a
few moments. Her mind began to work, but slowly, as
if it were half frozen. She realised she was in a room.

Presently, she noticed a man sitting on a chair,
staring at her. He had a glass in his hand. She tried to
probe his mind; but she was too weak; and, anyway,
there was a fog all over his thoughts. Vaguely she
wondered what he was drinking. Then she wondered
how long he had been drinking.

There were whisperings in her head. Weak, exhausted
whisperings. She recognised the pattern. Poor Dugal.
They must be working him very hard at Random Hill.
He was their best now, and they were driving him into
the ground.

'Vanessa,' came the tired whispering, 'dear Vanessa,
where are you? I'm so tired, but Dr. Lindemann keeps
asking me to send ... Vanessa, just say you are alive,
just for me. I won't tell ... I won't ...'

She felt a great surge of pity. Dr. Lindemann's
supply of chocolate bars was caught up in the law of
diminishing returns. She wondered if she, too, had the
strength to send. She gathered herself to try.

'Dugal, I'm all right,' she flashed weakly. 'Don't try

to trace. Just pretend — unless they have a monitor. I don't want to come back. Love and kisses. Out.'

'You will come back,' whispered a new pattern, strange and uneven, wavering in strength. 'You will come back, Vanessa. We shall find you.'

Who was that? It might have been Meriona. More likely it was Thomas, a thirteen-year-old, whose powers varied enormously. Vanessa remembered that one of the scientists had said Thomas ought to be good, when he had emotionally settled down after puberty.

Instantly she closed her mind, and tried a music block. But the man in the chair was speaking to her, and she had to listen to what he was saying. She was too weak to set up a block and, at the same time, find out what was going on.

"What is your name?" asked the man thickly. "Where have you come from? What the hell were you doing in my chicken run? What's wrong with you?"

She looked at him for a moment or two and said nothing, being unable to think of anything to say.

"Talk, girl!" he shouted. "Tell! I've had a bellyful of adolescent females." He poured himself another drink with trembling hands. "I have to decide whether to get the police or the psychiatric squad. So tell it for real."

Tears trickled down Vanessa's cheeks. It looked as if her luck had run out. She tried to think.

"Have you got any music?" she asked.

"Have I got any what?"

"Music. I need it in my head. I know it sounds stupid, but please play some music, and then I can talk." She knew she could not maintain her own blocks much longer. Music would help.

He shrugged. "You're nuts." He laughed. "So am I. So are we all. Yes, I have some taped music. What is your poison?"

39

"The 1812?" she asked hopefully. The sheer volume would help to disorientate any probes.

He seemed to understand. "I have it. You want all, or just the bangs?"

"The bangs. Repeated if possible."

"Can do."

He got up unsteadily from his chair and went to the music player that nestled compactly in a corner of the room. Vanessa could not see what he was dialling; but in a few seconds the thunderous sequences of the 1812 crashed through the room. He turned down the volume slightly.

"Now, acid head, the answers."

She had had a little time to think. "My name is Elizabeth Winter. I have run away from an orphanage. I was trying to steal food when I fainted, I suppose . . ." She looked at him appealingly. "Must you bring the police? I'll go away and promise not to give you any more trouble."

He gave a dreadful laugh and thrust the side of his face close to hers. She saw the scar tissue, the patches of pink flesh, the unnatural wrinkles, angry, livid.

"My name is Genghis Khan, and I eat girls who tell lies. Now, the truth, girl. You are in no position to play clever."

The 1812 rose to crescendos of cannon, trumpets and tympani. Vanessa gazed at the man's face, terrified. His eyes were wild. He might be a maniac. She wondered if she could try telergetic hypnosis. No, not like this. Not in this condition, and not with a subject filled with anger and whisky. But, also, she dared not tell him the truth.

"Well, girl?" His voice cut through the noisy music like a knife.

Weakly, with the tears coursing down her face, Vanessa tried again, knowing that it wouldn't work.

"I have told you the truth. I ran away."

"So you ran away. From what did you run away?"

"From an orphanage."

He hit her. He hit her face. The pain did not matter. The shock did.

"You are a telepath," he said. "You picked the wrong man, girlie. I know about telepaths. You wanted music as a block, so you couldn't send and couldn't be probed. Well, clever one, how am I doing?"

It was the end. Vanessa knew it was the end. She was too tired, too hungry, too weak to care. Vaguely, she wondered what the punishment would be when she was sent back. That did not seem to matter, either.

"You are doing fine," she managed to say. "My name is Vanessa Smith and I ran away from Random Hill, a school for paranormals. You may even get a reward for turning me in ... Have you anything to eat, please?"

He went back to his chair. There was a look of triumph on his face. He poured himself some more whisky.

"Well, child, we begin to understand each other. So you are one of the nation's gifted children. How interesting. But let us play fair. Parity of opportunity. I am Roland Badel, doctor of psychology. No, erase. Exdoctor of psychology. I was made ex by a cunning and rather delightful girl just about your age. At the time, I was quite cut up about it, as I recollect."

Vanessa didn't know what he was talking about or, indeed, if the words he uttered made any sense. But she managed to say: "I'm sorry. Have you anything to eat?"

"Have I anything to eat?" The superior smile on his face faded as he remembered how he had found her, unconscious with two smashed eggs in her hand. "Forgive me. Wretched hospitality. I have been alone too much. What would you like?"

"Milk?" asked Vanessa hopefully. "Bread?"

"Milk and bread," he said contritely. "Also bacon, eggs, fish — what would you like most of all?"

The room was wavering. He was wavering. The 1812 was wavering.

"Most of all," said Vanessa, "I would like to die."

Then the blessed darkness came, and she had nothing to worry about any more.

7

JENNY PARGETTER SAT at a table in the American Bar at the old Dorchester, sipping a gin and tonic moodily. Simon had promised to meet her at six o'clock. It was now ten minutes past. At half past they were supposed to take a French oil executive and his wife to early dinner before going on to the theatre.

When he had called on the V-phone, Simon said he had some news about Vanessa. He didn't have time to give it then because he was on his way to some wretched conference. If he didn't come soon, the French couple would arrive; and then Jenny would have to sit through dinner, polite conversation, a boring play, more polite conversation and late drinks before her curiosity could be satisfied. She hoped the Frenchman did not want to go on to a night club. So many of these visiting executives did. It was almost a conditioned reflex.

Jenny looked round the bar and sighed. A couple of tri-di personalities were chatting up a perfectly revolting girl who probably had pots of money. An aged actor was quietly and systematically getting himself stoned on Scotch. A striking Indian woman in a gold and red sari was listening attentively to the loud bad jokes of an ugly fat man who seemed familiar but could well be anything from a diamond merchant to a South American dictator. And scattered around were small groups of suburbanites pretending they were living it up.

Soon the Dorchester would be demolished — to make way for something hideous and half a mile high. Park Lane would never be the same again.

Jenny's reverie was broken by Simon's arrival. It was now twenty past six.

"Sorry I'm late, darling. Last minute idiocies. Shall I get you another drink?"

"We don't have time," she said despondently. "What about Vanessa?"

"The good news first Jean Baptiste has been called back to Paris. The evening is ours."

Jenny smiled with relief. "Allah is merciful. Yes, I will have another drink. A large one."

Simon signalled a waiter.

"Is it bad news about Vanessa?"

"No, not really. I persuaded the company to let me have one of our best espeople for a couple of days, a man named Draco. He went to the Richmond Children's Home, where you left the baby, and met with a blank wall. No record, they said, of a Vanessa Smith."

Jenny spilled her drink. "My God! There has to be."

"Quite. But no public record. Draco displayed folding money, but it didn't work. Then, on his way out, he flash-probed a dear old soul who looked as if she had been working there a million years."

"What does flash-probed mean?"

"He splashed her mind with what he knew about Vanessa, which wasn't much, and then listened for echoes. Incredibly the old girl remembered the year, remembered the baby, remembered you. So Draco went back to the front office and threatened them with tri-di, the press, habeas corpus, criminal investigation, questions in the House, and anything else he could think of.

44

They wilted — unofficially. It seems that Vanessa stayed there until she was seven years old. Then, apparently, the Department of Human Resources sent psych squads to all the orphanages in the country to pick up any potential paranormals for intensive training. Vanessa had a high esrate. So she was taken to a special school, a place called Random Hill. Draco went to Random Hill and talked to a Doctor Lindemann. He tried to pull the same bluff as at Richmond, but Lindemann wasn't buying. He denied Vanessa's existence, claimed to be covered by the Official Secrets Act and threatened to call the fuzz if Draco didn't depart at Mach Three."

"So the trail is lost, then?"

"No. Draco is a persistent creature. He is well paid for his persistence — among other things. He waited outside the perimeter — an electrified fence, by the way — until he saw kids playing in the grounds. Then he flash-probed once more. He got a response, but it was cut off quickly." Simon drank deeply of his own gin and tonic, "Sweet Jeez, I needed that."

"What did Draco learn?" Jenny gripped her fingers until the knuckles were white.

"Only that she had recently gone over the fence. Nobody seems to know if she is alive or dead."

"She is alive," said Jenny. "Dammit, how many dreams have I had since that night? Do you remember the time I got up and ate raw eggs because I told you I was starving." Her voice had risen.

"Take it easy, sweet. People are beginning to look at us."

"And the time I screamed," cried Jenny, unheeding, "because I saw a man whose face had been mutilated?"

"Jenny, pull yourself together. They'll throw us out."

"Vanessa is alive," said Jenny. "I know she is. But

she needs help. What can I do, Simon? Oh, God, what can I do?"

Sir Joseph Humboldt, Prime Minister of the United Kingdom, strolled in the garden at Number Ten Downing Street with Richard Haynes, his First Private Secretary, and half a dozen paras. The presence of the paranormals — two sensitives, one rapport, two blockers and a seeker — were necessary even when Sir Joseph was only admiring his roses. One never knew when some ambitious agent might try to probe the mind of the Prime Minister.

"Well, Dick, what do you think of that for a Western Sun?" Sir Joseph paused by a bush laden with great golden blooms.

"Magnificent, sir." Haynes was well aware of the great pride the Prime Minister took in the fact that he always found time to tend his own roses. He tried a frail joke and instantly regretted it. "Even the Opposition will allow that you have green fingers."

The Rt. Hon. Thomas Green, M.P., was the leader of the New Consensus Party; and in the current session Sir Joseph had given him a fair pounding, chiefly on the recent Security of the State Bill, by which the government reserved the right to recruit, enlist, commandeer all persons of known paranormal talent for the protection of the state.

Sir Joseph, being in a good mood, laughed. "Something might be made of that. Work it up and try it on our friends of the press. They will need such trifles to fill their pages in the silly season."

"Yes, sir." Haynes realised that he had got off lightly. Sir Joseph had the knack of delivering a compliment like a forearm smash.

The two men, with their retinue of paras, passed a

single bush that displayed red, white and blue roses. It was the gift of the President of France. Sir Joseph looked at the bush and sniffed. He did not care for the French President. He was amazed that the bush was doing so well.

"What about Professor Raeder?" he asked abruptly.

"I have no news, sir. Security forces are on maximum alert."

"I want him dead," said Sir Joseph. "I don't care how it is done, but I want him dead. Let it be known."

"Yes, sir."

"Only because he wants me dead," went on the Prime Minister. "As a private person I could accept risks. But as the king's First Minister, I cannot. You understand?"

"Yes, sir."

"Then see to it, Dick. Get those well-paid security people off their fat backsides. Dammit, the man is mortal. He exists, and he exists in the United Kingdom. If our people cannot take him out, they are not worth their salt."

"Yes sir ... Sir, you have a Parliamentary Question." Haynes took a House of Commons order paper from his pocket and began to read: "Question twenty-three: To ask the Prime Minister if he can assure the House that Vanessa Smith, a British citizen, is not being restrained forcibly at Random Hill Residential School, an institution for children of paranormal talents, against her will."

Sir Joseph stopped by a spendid rose bush bowed under the weight of a large number of full red blooms. He plucked one of the best and gave it to his Secretary. "Put that in your lapel, Dick. It's a beauty." He gazed distastefully at a neighbouring bush of Papa Meilland, also laden with blooms. "Far superior to this French

47

crap ... Vanessa Smith? Who the devil is Vanessa Smith?"

"She is an orphan, sir. Seventeen years old. A paranormal of exceptional powers."

"Tom Green is having his fun, I suppose. Wants to show that I am pre-empting the Bill? Well, what about this Vanessa Smith? Is she at Random Hill? Can we produce her? Will she say that she is having a fine time and loves everybody?"

Haynes swallowed, and fumbled with the rose he had just been given. "Sir, she was at Random Hill, but we cannot produce her. She went over the wall."

"Christ Jesus!" the Prime Minister exploded. "If she does exist, and we can't produce her to say that all is lovely, my Bill falls flat on its tiny. What answer have you drafted?"

Dick Haynes brought another piece of paper from his pocket. "His Majesty's Government has no knowledge of the person referred to as Vanessa Smith. However, enquiries are being pursued, and information will be given to the House as soon as it is obtained. His Majesty's Government assumes that the question has been asked in good faith and that the person named is not an invention of political imagination."

Sir Joseph thought for a moment or two. "That is either very weak or very strong. Events will decide which. Find this Vanessa Smith very soon, and have her say the right things. If she won't say the right things, arrange an accident. If you can't find her, expunge the records. She never existed. Is that clear?"

"Perfectly, sir."

"I smell Raeder in this business," said Sir Joseph irritably. "It is the sort of thing he would feed to Tom Green. Yes, I smell Raeder... Get security moving,

Dick. And if they take out this Vanessa Smith as well, I shall not complain. The dead are usually less embarrassing than the living."

"Yes, sir."

"Roses," said Sir Joseph, sniffing at a Marilyn Monroe, "are a great consolation."

8

VANESSA WOKE UP screaming. She sat upright — not knowing where she was — with sweat dripping from her forehead and tears rolling down her cheeks, and screamed uncontrollably in the semi-darkness, remembering the nightmares, phantoms, and cacophony of insistent voices that seemed to have transformed her mind into a psychic waste land.

Suddenly the room was flooded with soft light, and the man with the disfigured face was sitting on the bed; and Vanessa found herself leaning against his chest, found her hair being stroked with slow, soothing motions, as she sobbed uncontrollably.

"Child, child," said Roland Badel gently, "calm down. Take it easy. I haven't sent for the fuzz. No one knows you are here. Relax."

"I'm not a child," sniffed Vanessa inconsequentially. "I'm practically a woman."

He laughed. "So you are. I have reason to know."

Then she realised that she was in a bed, between soft clean sheets, and wearing nothing but a man's shirt that was far too big for her.

She shivered, then felt her face burning with embarrassment.

"Should I have left you in wet clothes? Should I have done nothing about the cuts and scratches on your body?" He held her hand. "Listen to me, Vanessa. Forgive me for drinking myself stupid, for being brutal ... You were quite a shock, you see. You reminded me of ... Well, that's a long story. Some other time ... I'm sober, now. Sober enough to realise that, in the state you were in, I must have seemed like something out of a peculiarly horrible nightmare. Forgive me. I have tried to atone by attending to the needs of the child. I did not touch the woman. Believe that ... Probe my mind, if you can, if you want to."

Vanessa shot a quick probe. His mind was open, waiting. What he had said was true. But she discovered more than that, much more.

"You confused me with Susan Stride," she said unsteadily. "The girl who tried to kill you. Now, you want to help me because you think of both of us as refugees. Also," she faltered, blushing again. "Also, you feel a kind of love."

"So now you must realise why people like me are afraid of people like you," he said. "You unnerve us. You make us naked." Again he laughed. "Which is more shocking — me undressing your body, or you undressing my mind?"

"I'm sorry," said Vanessa contritely. "It was by invitation. I won't do it again, unless you allow me, or unless ..."

"Unless you think I will betray you?"

She nodded. "Is that unreasonable?"

"No." He smiled. "Remember only that I can feel a probe. I give you that information free of charge. Incidentally, don't worry about the love element. I can contain it. I will try not to offend you."

"What are you going to do — about me?"

"Do you want to probe again?"

"No. I'm just asking."

51

"Well, then. I'm going to look after you, feed you, help you get back your strength."

"And afterwards?"

"Afterwards? Refugees like us, Vanessa, find it difficult to consider an abstraction called afterwards. We live from hour to hour, day to day."

Suddenly, Vanessa stiffened. The nightmare voices had returned. They were somehow nibbling away at her mind. She set up a block, but she did not have much strength.

"What is it?"

"They are trying to probe me," she said as calmly as possible. "Could you let me have some music, please? I can't stop them alone."

He did not say anything. He got up from the bed, went to a chest of drawers, found a transistor radio, switched it on, turned the volume up.

Vintage pop music flooded the room. Vanessa was immensely grateful. She relaxed her block and let the music dominate her mind.

"Why are they so persistent?" He had to speak loudly to make himself heard above the music.

"I don't know."

"Are you so good?"

"The best they had, I think. But at other schools there must be many who are as good, or better."

Badel stroked his chin. "Not so many as you think, perhaps. Paranormals — the good ones — are much in demand these days ... Did they let you see much tri-di at Random Hill?"

"Quite a lot. It was censored."

"Then you may not know that Joe Humboldt is fascinated by paranormals. Just now, they are the in thing. The Prime Minister needs them for political insurance, therefore he is afraid of them." He laughed grimly. "The political animal reasons thus: who is not with us is against us... Perhaps that is why they want you back so much. Perhaps you are — or could be — a valuable weapon in the psych war."

"I don't want to take part in any kind of war," she said vehemently. "I just want to be left in peace... It is not only the Random Hill people who are trying to find out where I am. I know their patterns. But there are other patterns, other probes. At first, I thought they were all working with the police, or something like that. But there is a sort of smell of evil about some of them, a smell of death." She shuddered. "They frighten me. They frighten me horribly... I'm so hungry. Could I have something to eat, please?"

He held her hand. "I have plenty of food waiting for you, my dear. Soup, milk, eggs, fish, meat — whatever you like. You shall have whatever you want in a minute or two. But let us think. Time may be critical. You want to be left in peace, and I want to be left in peace. Our interests are identical... I told you my name. Do you remember it?"

"Yes, it's — "

"Don't say it. Don't even think it. What I told you was a pack of lies. Now I will tell you the truth. My real name is Oliver Anderson. I was injured in a hover-car collision. I used to be a painter. Perhaps, when I have fully recovered, I will paint again... What is my name?"

"Oliver Anderson."

"Where do I live?"

"I — I don't know."

"You really don't know?"

"No. I just ran and ran. I don't know where I am."

"Good. Then I shall not tell you. You must know as little as possible. What is my name?"

"Oliver Anderson."

"What am I?"

"A painter. You were injured in a hovercar crash."

"You had better believe it," he said intensely. "Because if you don't, I shall beat you. What is my name?"

"Oliver Anderson." Tears trickled down her face. "I'm so hungry. Please may I have some food?"

"Say: please, Oliver, may I have something to eat?"

"Please, Oliver, may I have something to eat?"

"That's better. Now lie back and rest for a minute or two."

Presently he brought soup and milk and bread and cold meat. She ate greedily until he forced her to eat slowly.

9

DENZIL INGRAM WAS a solid extrovert, a pragmatist, a professional hunter. He was also highly intelligent and, as head of the Snatch Group in the Department of Internal Security, politically powerful. He had a P2 rating, which gave him — if he needed it — direct access to Sir Joseph Humboldt.

Because of a certain question asked in the House of Commons, he had taken personal control of the team assigned to tracing Vanessa Smith. He was now in the process of causing Dr. Lindemann to sweat profusely.

"You were personally responsible for the training, welfare and security of the girl?"

"Yes, sir." There was no way Lindemann could wriggle out of that responsibility. It was all on paper.

"You clever boys make me sick," observed Ingram coldly. "Here you are, running a classified factory farm for child paras, and all the security precautions you can develop are electrified fences, guards and dogs."

"Security is not my responsibility."

"But Vanessa Smith is. You should have known, Lindemann. Even allowing for your Ph.D., you should have known when the girl was going to run. An ordinary prison guard would have known. There's a remoteness in the eyes, an air of evasiveness, a sense of detachment. It always adds up to escape."

"I am not a prison guard," retorted Dr. Lindemann. "I am a scientist."

"Before this little jape is over," said Ingram, "you may well be a reconditioned lavatory cleaner . . . Well, let us see how we stand now. You have now destroyed all records of the girl's existence?"

"Yes."

"You are sure?"

"Of course I'm sure — sir."

"Good. Because, Lindemann, if there is anything on paper, micro-film or in computer storage that proves she existed, I, personally, will stamp on your balls. At the moment, we are on a no-win basis. Therefore we must play for a draw. If we could find her within the next twenty-four hours, and if she would say the right things, there is a clear win. But my nose tells me that we won't get her in twenty-four hours and, even if we did, there would not be enough time to brainwash her for public display. Therefore we are left with negatives. We must ensure that the Opposition doesn't find her before we do. And when we find her, we must quietly take her out."

"Why has she become so important?" asked Lindemann. "She is highly gifted, but there are other highly gifted children. She is not irreplaceable."

Ingram sighed. "Wrong again, college boy. She is not just Vanessa Smith. She is now a Parliamentary Question. Sir Joseph Humboldt does not like Parliamentary Questions where he cannot score . . . Now, let us quietly review progress. A farmer saw her stealing eggs. A chopper reported her heading south. What is your contribution?"

Dr. Lindemann pressed an intercom switch. "Send in Dugal, please."

The door opened and Dugal Nemo came into the

56

office. He looked very small. His face was pale, his eyes bloodshot.

Dr. Lindemann brought a chocolate bar out of a drawer in his desk. Denzil Ingram saw the look on the boy's face and rolled his eyes upwards. "Put the chocolate away, Lindemann. It will make the boy vomit. Can't you see he's not one of your Pavlovian dogs?" He turned to Dugal.

"Now, laddie, what is your name?"

"Dugal Nemo, sir."

"Do you like this place?"

"Yes, sir."

"Do they treat you well?'

"Yes, sir."

"Do you like Vanessa?"

"Yes, sir."

"Would you like her to come back? Would you like things to be as they were before she ran away?"

"Yes, sir. Very much. I love Vanessa and she loves me."

"Well, laddie, then we can help each other. I want Vanessa back, too. I don't love her like you do, you understand. But I think I might like her — when I get to know her. I want to meet her, you see. I want to understand what made her run away. If I can, I'll put it right. That's a promise. Now, what do you know?"

"Not very much, sir. Dr. Lindemann has asked me to do a lot of probing recently. It has made me very tired. I can't seem to get the patterns right. Perhaps I will do better if I can have a good rest."

Ingram shot a despairing glance at Lindemann then turned to Dugal once more. "I'm sorry about that, Dugal. Dr. Lindemann is going to let you have a good rest after we have talked. Now, what do you know?"

Dugal hesitated. "Please, sir, will Vanessa get into trouble?"

Ingram patted his head. "No, laddie. We won't do anything to make her unhappy. We want to make sure she is safe and well, that's all. You see, she is important to us as well as to you. So we are all on the same side."

Dugal brightened. "I'm glad. Vanessa will be glad, too. I'll send as soon as I can."

"You know where she is, boy?"

"No, sir. But I know how she is. She is very hungry and very tired. I think she's been ill. She doesn't want to come back."

"How do you know?"

"She told me."

Dr. Lindemann opened his mouth and looked as if he were about to explode. Ingram withered him with a glance.

"She told you?"

"Yes, sir. It was very weak, but she did send. Since then I have only heard music blocks . . . But I tried once when she must have been sleeping. There was frightening shapes in her mind. Somebody else was there, too. I felt him. Very cold . . . I got scared and came out."

Ingram, who understood little of telepathic processes, made the best of it he could. "You are sure there was someone else?"

"Yes, sir."

"Can you describe him, tell us about him?"

Dugal smiled. "You can't describe a probe, sir. It's warm or it's cold, that's all. This one was cold. Too cold."

"Too cold for what?"

"Too cold to be good," said Dugal innocently. "That is the way it was."

58

Ingram tried again. "The music. Can you tell us anything about that?"

"The first time, it was very loud and with lots of bangs. They sounded like guns. I think I have heard it before, but I don't know where."

"And the second time?"

Dugal wrinkled his nose. "Oldies. Classic Pop. Country and Western. Folk. Even the Beatles. Terrible stuff. All out of the ark."

"Is that all you can tell us?"

Dugal scratched his head. "I don't know, sir. I'm not sure."

"What are you not sure about?"

"I keep thinking about a man who has something wrong with his face."

"Is he connected with Vanessa? Does she know him?"

"I don't know, sir. Maybe it is just something I made up — you know, like a nightmare. I've been trying to reach Vanessa an awful long time . . ." A tear trickled down his face. "She doesn't want to talk to me. Can I go, now? I'm very tired."

"Yes, son. Go and get some rest. Dr. Lindemann won't need you at least until tomorrow."

Jenny Pargetter had just listened to the 1812 Overture for the third time. She didn't know why, because it was not a piece of music she liked. It was too flashy, too naïve. But when she heard it — particularly when the cannon started booming away — she derived a strange feeling of security. It was as if she needed the noise in order to be able to think freely. Which was plainly ridiculous. Thinking was best done without distraction. But, while she waited for Simon to come home, she indulged herself idiotically by filling the room with sound.

For once, he came home early. He kissed her, glanced at the stereo box, raised an eyebrow, and turned the volume down.

"Love, how can you stand it?"

Jenny looked at him, puzzled. "I don't know, Simon. I don't even like it. But it makes me feel good."

"May I turn it off?"

She got up from the settee. "Yes. I don't need it now that you are here."

"Why did you need it?"

She seemed almost surprised by the question. "So that I could think. It provides a good background for thinking . . . Strange. I'd never thought of the 1812 before as an aid to thinking."

Simon poured himself a large drink, a lot of whisky and a little water. "Would you like one, Jenny? I think maybe you are going to need it."

"You have bad news?"

"I don't know whether it is good or bad." Simon swallowed half his drink. Then he topped up his own glass and poured a neat whisky for Jenny. "There was a Parliamentary Question this afternoon. Tom Green asked the P.M. if he could assure the House that Vanessa Smith was not being restrained against her will at Random Hill Residential School."

Jenny swallowed her whisky in one. "What did Black Joe say?"

"He denied that she existed. It was a stalling action."

"I see. Give me another whisky. It seems your Mr. Draco was right." Jenny began to laugh. "Marvellous, isn't it? My child is now a matter of national importance. She has gone over the wall to the embarrassment of H.M. Government." Jenny's laughter dissolved in tears. "I wish I'd known her. I wish I'd kept her. Oh, God, I wish I'd looked after her!"

Simon held her close. "Steady, love. We cannot change the past. I am as much to blame as you ... But we must face facts as they now are. Wherever Vanessa is now, she is in great danger.

"Because," went on Simon, holding her tight enough to hurt, "Humboldt will need to prove his statement. Otherwise, his Security of the State Bill might get hammered. So, somehow, we must find Vanessa first."

Professor Marius Raeder fed Turkish delight to the child he called Quasimodo. Quasimodo's real name was Hubert Fisher. He was twelve years old; but his body was misshapen and his personality warped. He looked like a wizened dwarf. Professor Raeder, sensing that the boy had been treated as an object of compassion for too long, treated him as an object of ridicule. He responded well. Since his escape from Coniston Residential School, his paranormal talents had increased prodigiously.

After the third chunk of Turkish delight, Professor Raeder sensed that the time was ripe for the experiment. A brown rat was happily nibbling at a pile of oatmeal in a small cage on the far side of the room.

"Kill," said Professor Raeder.

Quasimodo, his lips sticky, and with a dribble of half-melted Turkish delight on his chin, looked at the Professor uncomprehendingly.

"Kill the rat," said Raeder. "If you can kill it, you get more of this dreadful stuff. Do you understand, Quasimodo?"

The boy nodded. He closed his eyes and concentrated. The rat fell on its side. But after a few seconds, it picked itself up and started to eat the oatmeal once more."

"Not good enough!" shouted Professor Raeder. "You are not good enough, Quasimodo. You can't kill a rat!"

Quasimodo ground his teeth in anger. Then he gave a great sigh, looked longingly at the box of Turkish delight that the Professor was holding, and closed his eyes once more. This time, the rat fell dead.

"Ha!" said Quasimodo triumphantly. "More now. You promised."

Professor Marius Raeder and his grotesque little companion were in a small room that had been converted into the Professor's study in a nineteenth-century house. It stood in a clearing in a deer forest in the North West Highlands of Scotland. From the air, the house was barely visible. Its roof and walls had been skilfully camouflaged; and a chopper pilot would have to be very observant and know what he was looking for in order to spot it.

Which suited Professor Raeder perfectly. And just in case the hypothetical chopper pilot became too curious and attempted to use his radio or investigate further, an automatic jammer would neutralise his transmission; and, if necessary, coned laser beams would burn him out of the sky.

Until two years before, Professor Raeder had occupied the chair of paranormal psychology at the University of Cambridge. He had been regarded as the foremost authority on this subject in Europe. He was on the point of being awarded the Nobel Prize for para-psychology for his research into the material effects of telergetic influences. Then Sir Joseph Humboldt came to political power. Professor Raeder was dismissed from his post ignominiously after a series of photographs showing him participating in a sex orgy had been released to the news media. The Nobel Prize was given to an American scientist for his researches into precognition; and Professor Raeder rapidly became — if only for a time — the most unwanted man in the United Kingdom.

The photographs had been faked. They had been faked by Sir Joseph Humboldt's agents. Professor Raeder was neither homosexual nor heterosexual. He just was not sexual — a fact which too many people found too hard to believe.

The photographs had been faked because Sir Joseph had a long memory, and was something of a connoisseur in the art of paying off old scores. He and Raeder had been at university together. In youth, each of them had been idealistic in his own fashion. The scholarly Marius Raeder had been a prominent member of a group of rather intellectual anarchists whose chief activity consisted of talking a great deal. Joseph Humboldt, ambitious and ruthless, was the leader of a neofascist student organisation whose aim was to dominate the Students' Union and, ultimately, the university itself. Humboldt and his companions were not averse to violence and had already terrorised two left-wing student groups into disintegration. Marius Raeder realised it would not be long before the small group of anarchists received the attention of Humboldt and his ruggerplaying zombies. He was ready for them.

The meetings of the anarchists, well publicised, took place regularly in the crypt of a disused church. When Joe Humboldt and his strong-arm boys arrived to break up a meeting and terrorise those present, Marius Raeder hastily retreated from the ensuing mêlée. He had work to do — with a camera. He took shots of the fracas. He recorded Humboldt's hearties beating up a short-sighted anarchist whose glasses had been deliberately stamped upon. He took a shot of a terrified girl student being forced to kiss Joe Humboldt's boots. He even captured the look of ecstasy on Humboldt's face when he realised that his attempt at demoralisation had totally succeeded.

Next day, prints of the photographs were on the Vice-Chancellor's desk. By the end of the week, Joseph Humboldt and those of his followers who could be identified were rusticated.

So, the Prime Minister had settled his score, and Professor Raeder had sought refuge in the Scottish Highlands. But the contest was not yet over. Professor Raeder had one great weapon to pit against the political might of the Prime Minister. And that weapon was paranormal psychology.

The deformed boy, Quasimodo, was one unit in a small team of outstanding paranormals with which Professor Raeder, now an embittered and vengeful old man, hoped not only to deal with Sir Joseph Humboldt once and for all but also to topple a government which had become a thinly disguised autocracy.

At Cambridge, in the course of his researches, Professor Raeder had access to the files of the most gifted young paranormals discovered by the Department of Human Resources. Several of the children whose case histories he had studied now lived and trained and, with Raeder's skilled assistance, extended their powers in this house that was discreetly hidden and well defended in the Scottish Highlands. Some had escaped from the special schools with Raeder's encouragement or help. Some had run away on their own initiative and had then been traced and recruited. Slowly and systematically they were all programmed to develop and combine techniques of psychological destruction.

There remained one person — or, more properly, one type of person — necessary to unite the talents of these gifted and perverted children so that they would become an effective death squad. That person — that type of person — must have the ability to receive simultaneously and handle simultaneously several different telesends. That person would be an extremely sensitive telepath, passive rather than aggressive. That person would have to be able to accept a total invasion of the mind.

Such a person was Vanessa. For some time, Professor Raeder's best pupils had been monitoring her uncontrolled transmissions. They knew when and how she had left Random Hill. They had been able to tap some of her experiences thereafter.

Professor Raeder pointed to another rat in a cage by the side of that containing the dead one.

"Kill," he commanded Quasimodo. This time there was no hesitation. Quasimodo was contented briefly with his intake of Turkish delight. He closed his eyes and concentrated, and the rat fell dead.

"Very good," said Professor Raeder. "Very good indeed. All we need now is the burning glass."

Quasimodo opened his eyes, and nodded vigorously. "Vanessa," he said with a knowing look. "Vanessa Smith. May I have some more Turkish delight?"

10

Vanessa recovered rapidly. She was young and re-silient. All she needed was rest, warmth and food. She got it. The man who had conditioned her to call him and think of him as Oliver saw to that. He could not do much to protect her against the frequency with which pleading, insistent, or malign voices entered her mind. She would have to look to her own psychic protection. But he could and did give her physical security. It was enough. She was grateful.

She was grateful even for the monotonous rigours of the conditioning process, the wearing sessions of question and answer. With painstaking attention to detail, he constructed an entirely new past for himself. The con-ditioning had to be faultless. He, too, had to be con-vinced of the credibility of his new persona.

One morning, while Vanessa was sleeping, he had taken the car he now used but rarely and had driven fifty miles to a town he had never before visited in his life. There he had bought a great quantity of artists' materials: canvas, oil paints, brushes, palette knives, an easel, sketch blocks, charcoal sticks, pastel colours and several books on advanced techniques. He had also bought a sheepskin jacket, shirts, trousers and country shoes for Vanessa — but nothing feminine.

When he returned to his cottage, he took the clothes

that Vanessa had arrived in and burned them. Then he began to turn one room of the house into a typical studio. While Vanessa watched in wonder, he deliberately spilled paints and turpentine on to the carpet and trod the colours in. Then he drank some whisky and sloshed quantities of colour on to a large piece of canvas board propped on the studio easel. Somehow, he managed to work the colour with a palette knife so that the final effect was of a primitive landscape, full of violence and mystery. The effect was pleasing or, at least, startling. He regarded it with pleasure. Then he daubed a ragged black line through it, flung the canvas board to one side, and started something else.

While he worked, he invented his past. He had a keen ear for accents and an ability to emulate them. Roland Badel had been born in the south of England, had a cultivated accent and a university education. But Roland Badel was to be put into suspended animation. Oliver Anderson was a northerner, coming from a poor family, and poorly educated. His parents had separated when he was quite young; and, though he had lived with his mother for a time, he had run away from home when he was sixteen. He had drifted for a time, working as a casual labourer for the money he needed to keep from starving. He had washed dishes in restaurants, helped build the monorail tracks that connected London with its four airports, mowed lawns for old ladies, worked as a roughneck on North Sea drilling rigs, picked apples in Devonshire orchards.

All these activities were things that a stranger called Dr. Roland Badel knew about intimately. His patients had told him. Therefore Oliver Anderson could create a past that was not too difficult for him to absorb.

When he was about twenty, he met a tramp who had a fantastic talent for painting. In a couple of hours, with the right materials, he could produce a Picasso, or a Modigliani, or a Klee, or a Van Gogh, or a Pollock that would confound the experts. (Dr. Badel, late psychologist, had encountered such a person who had served ten years for art forgeries). It was from this tramp that Oliver Anderson learned to appreciate the magic of colour, the occult beauty of line.

As he tackled another canvas and talked to the amazed girl who sat watching him, Badel found himself slipping into his new role easily. The northern accent with its short *a* and its lost *h* seemed to come quite naturally. He found that he enjoyed painting. Perhaps he should have been a painter, a real one ...

"What's me name, love?"

"Oliver." The response was now automatic.

"Oliver what, you girt bitch?"

"Oliver Anderson."

"Where did I meet you?"

"London. I was mainlining. You got me off it."

"That's right. I got you off it for the screws, you understand. Nothing personal."

"Yes, Oliver, you got me off it for the screws." To Vanessa, it was still an unreal game. "Am I good enough in bed then?"

He looked at her calmly. "I've had better, and I've had worse. You'll do for the time being."

Vanessa laughed. He hit her.

"Put on some music, you stupid child. Play anything that will block you. Understand?"

Tears trickled down her face, Vanessa nodded dumbly. She selected the 1812 once more. The cannons seemed to be shooting straight at her.

He came and held her close. "Listen, little one. The charade is for real. We are trying to ensure that they cannot trace you through me. You don't know where you are, but you do know who you are with. Let them steal that information while you are sleeping, relaxed, unguarded, and the air will be black with Security choppers . . . Who am I?"

"Oliver Anderson." She wiped away the tears and smiled. "Probably the worst painter in the United Kingdom."

"Misunderstood," he said, in his best northern accent, "just misunderstood. I'm ahead of my time, love. Not to worry. Posterity will accord me the honour that is due."

"I love you," said Vanessa, as the cannon crashed loud. "You really care about me. You are the first *adult* to really care about me. I love you."

He kissed her. "Darling Vanessa, I love you also, as you well know. But try to remember that you are supposed to be here just for the screws. Unless you can be sure of your blocks — and you can't — you must think of me as a rather crude middle-aged failure still thinking he can make the big time, as they say in stone-age movies. I'm good for a bed and food and a few handouts, but not much else. You are simply using me and waiting until you can steal enough money to get across to France, or Germany or Denmark. If you are as good as I think you are, the people who are trying to trace you will be utterly ruthless. They will stop at nothing to get you back or take you out. It will help if they think you are planning to leave the country."

"Take me out?" Vanessa did not understand.

"It means kill, love. Very probably, if they think you could be an embarrassment, they will try to kill you."

She was amazed. "Why should anyone want to kill me?"

He sighed. "Until you came along, I didn't want to have anything to do with the rest of the world. As you know, I have no tri-di, no V-phone. I have taped music and a transistor radio that I never used. But, since you came, I began to listen to the newscasts. There was a Parliamentary Question about you, Vanessa. Sir Joseph Humboldt didn't like it. He was of the implied opinion that you don't exist. There will be few people who want to prove him wrong, and a number of highly trained specialists who will be well paid to prove him right. Do I make myself clear?"

Vanessa shuddered. "I'm frightened. I'm so frightened. I didn't realise that — "

The 1812 came to an end.

Oliver Anderson said: "Don't worry, love. Oliver will take care of you. Just open your legs at the right time, and strike a few quasi-erotic poses as required, and you've got it made."

Vanessa gazed at him, and forced herself to see only a middle-aged fourth-rate painter.

Many miles away, Dugal Nemo received her impression and reported it.

Farther away still, so did Quasimodo.

11

DENZIL INGRAM SAT nursing the gin and tonic that
Simon Pargetter had just poured for him. Jenny, sitting
opposite him, also with a gin and tonic, tried to appear
calm and detached, but could not disguise her anxiety.
Her eyes were bright — too bright — and she could not
keep still.

Ingram's trained mind came up with the answer:
drugs or, just possibly, prescribed sedatives and
emotional trauma. She knew something. If she didn't
tell it, she would have to be probed. Normally, Ingram
would have left this kind of follow-up to a junior; but
the stakes had suddenly become high.

The Opposition seemed to think they had a sporting
chance of using the case of Vanessa Smith to force a
defeat on the Security of the State Bill. If that happened, the Prime Minister could fall. He had not yet
mustered quite enough backing to assume dictatorial
powers. Sir Joseph Humboldt, the prospect of absolute
power almost within his grasp, was not a man to pre-
varicate. The word had come down that if Ingram could
take out Vanessa before the Opposition got a line on
her, he would be well rewarded — a knighthood possibly, financial benefits certainly, also the prospect of
advancement even, perhaps, to Security Control. If, on

the other hand, he failed, he could only expect total professional disaster.

So Denzil Ingram was delegating as little as possible of the investigation to other hands.

"Mrs. Pargetter," he said, "I really am sorry to have to trouble you. But it is important. Do you have any knowledge of the whereabouts of your daughter?"

She drank her gin and tonic in one. "She doesn't exist," said Jenny in a shrill voice. "According to Sir Joseph Humboldt, there is no such person as Vanessa Smith."

Ingram shrugged. "Bureaucracy. You know what records are like. In this automatic world of ours, computers sometimes spit out idiocies."

Jenny looked at Simon. "Give me another drink, please."

"Yes, darling. But remember you have had your pills."

"Pills?" said Ingram. "I'm sorry. I didn't know you were ill, Mrs. Pargetter."

"Sedatives," said Simon quickly. "My wife has been rather tense recently. And this business doesn't help. You understand?"

"I do indeed. I'm very sorry that I have to bother her at such a time... Mrs. Pargetter, do you know where Vanessa is?"

"She's nowhere," answered Jenny, thickly. "Black Joe says so, and he always tells the truth... Do you know what I did this afternoon, Mr. Ingram? No, of course you don't. I went to Somerset House to check on her birth entry. It wasn't there."

"The system isn't perfect," said Ingram. "No doubt Sir Joseph's young men had similar difficulties. Perhaps that accounts for the answer he gave in the House."

"Please don't treat me like an idiot," said Jenny, her face white. "You know that Vanessa exists. You traced me. Why didn't you tell Joe Humboldt she exists?"

"Parliamentary matters are not my concern, Mrs. Pargetter. It is only my duty to find Vanessa if possible, and see that no harm comes to her. Can you help me?"

Jenny downed the second gin and tonic. "Help you! You are one of Black Joe's men. I wouldn't help you to find a taxi."

"Please excuse her, Mr. Ingram," said Simon anxiously. "This is a trying time. My wife, as you can see, is under some stress. Perhaps you could come back tomorrow morning? I'm sure Jenny will feel better then."

"I'm sorry, sir. Time is important to us, as you will appreciate."

Jenny gave a brittle laugh. "I have just thought of something. We still live in a democracy. Humboldt can't have it all his own way yet. I'll call a press conference and tell everybody that I'm Vanessa's mother. I'll tell them all I know, and — "

"Just what do you know, Mrs. Pargetter?" Ingram struck like a snake.

Simon, alert to all the implications, cast a despairing look at his wife. Jenny was in no mood for caution.

"Attend the press conference, and find out."

Ingram sighed. "There will be no press conference, Mrs. Pargetter. If there were, you would simply be discredited as a neurotic woman. Officially, your daughter does not exist. But there will be no press conference."

Simon put a hand on Jenny's shoulder, trying to reassure her, trying to calm her, trying to restrain her. But she was in no mood for restraint.

Again she laughed. "I am a free citizen. I have

committed no crime. Try and stop me. Let us see who will be discredited."

Even before she had finished speaking, Denzil Ingram pressed a button on a small electronic device he had in his pocket. He was not happy. This was going to be one of those jobs where everything had to be done the hard way.

Simon Pargetter, not knowing that it was already too late, did his best to avert the collision. "My wife is overwrought, Mr. Ingram. Perhaps if I were to talk to her alone for a few minutes, it would — " He never completed his sentence.

There was a noise at the door, a dull plop. Then the door opened and four men burst into the flat. When they saw Denzil Ingram sitting calmly in his chair, they stood still, as if awaiting orders. Jenny gazed at them open-mouthed. Simon seemed numbed.

"Mr. Pargetter," said Ingram, "I really am sorry about this, but your wife's attitude leaves me no choice. I cannot afford to take risks."

"What are these men doing here?" stormed Jenny. "Get them out! Get them out of my home! I'm going to bring a criminal charge against you for this."

"Jenny, *please*. You're making it worse." Simon Pargetter had enough grip on reality to know what was happening.

Denzil Ingram stood up. "Mrs. Pargetter, I am taking you and your husband into protective custody. You will both be well looked after in comfortable surroundings. Perhaps you would like to pack a few things."

"Protective custody!" Jenny screamed. "Who are these people — Black Joe's thugs?" She flung her empty glass at him. Her aim was good, and Ingram was caught by surprise. The glass shattered on his forehead, leaving a small cut.

74

Jeez, I'm getting old, he told himself. You can never tell with women. One of the snatch team had drawn a gun. Ingram motioned to him to put it away. Then he took out a handkerchief and dabbed at the blood he felt trickling down towards his left eye.

"Mrs. Pargetter, I am convinced you know something about Vanessa. It may be important, or it may not. You will have to be probed."

"You can't do that," said Simon angrily. "You don't have the power."

Ingram gave a faint smile. "You would be amazed to know what powers I have, Mr. Pargetter. You really would. Now, let's not waste any more time."

Dr. Lindemann broke the ampoule and quickly filled his hypodermic syringe. Dugal sat passively on the chair, staring out through the window. There were dark circles round his eyes. A growing child needs quite a lot of sleep. Dugal had had very little during the past three days.

Lindemann was not naturally callous. He knew that the boy was near to exhaustion; and he had tried to use some of his other star paranormals to ease the burden. But Dugal, he knew, was the only one who could effectively reach Vanessa. Dugal, at his best, and with the will, could pass all her blocks and go in deep.

The scientist knew now that his professional future depended on producing results. He, certainly, was not unaware of the extraordinary powers of Denzil Ingram. He was sorry for Dugal. But, in a matter of survival, the ancient law obtained : *sauve qui peut*.

Dugal knew what Dr. Lindemann was doing. But he did not want to see the needle. It was natural. The effect of the injection had been explained to him — as

75

well as it is possible to explain a complicated bio-chemical process to a small child.

He knew that he was going to get a shot of a wonder drug called Amplia Nine. Dr. Lindemann had told him that it would make him feel full of energy, full of life, that it would destroy tiredness and make him feel that he could do anything he wanted to do.

What Dr. Lindemann had not told him was that Amplia Nine — a spin-off from hallucinogenic research — would temporarily amplify his mental talents. Also Dr. Lindemann neglected to inform him that this short-term magnification of his natural abilities would eventually be paid for by the destruction of several million of his brain cells.

Research has shown that one shot of Amplia Nine would reduce the Intelligence Quotient of an average person by five to seven points. A second shot would reduce it by eight to fifteen points. A third shot would produce, in the end, a moron.

"Well, Dugal?"

"I'm ready, Dr. Lindemann." Dugal held out his arm, but still looked out through the window. "You promise it will help Vanessa?"

"Yes, I promise." Lindemann pressed the needle into the boy's arm.

Dugal flinched, but he did not complain.

"For the next hour," said Dr. Lindemann, "you will feel a little drowsy. But after that you will be wide awake and stronger than you have ever been before. When that happens, I want you to concentrate on reaching Vanessa. She may have blocks, but I don't think they will bother you. I want you to go in deep and find out everything you can. Remember, we need to know where she is, we need to know if she is safe, we want to help her."

Dugal yawned. His arm was itching somewhat, but it did not seem to matter.

"I'll probe her," he said. "But can I talk to her?"

"Talk to her?"

"Explain that we all want to help her."

Dr. Lindemann smiled. "Talk to her, by all means, Dugal. But remember that she may not believe what you say. Personally, I think that she has been very ill. The important thing is for you to remember everything. Do you understand?"

Dugal yawned once more. "I understand, Dr. Lindemann. But will Vanessa understand?"

Professor Raeder was in a didactic mood. He confronted his small group of paranormals as if they were students in tutorial — which, perhaps, they were.

But, such students! Quasimodo, childish, yet telepathetically lethal; Janine, twenty years old and the oldest in the group, a voyeur nymphomaniac and a probe of quite exceptional powers; Alfred, seventeen, a rawboned youth and an extrovert who could break almost any block or throw up a wall that would stop anyone, including Janine; Robert, eleven, whose powers of telepathic suggestion were, as far as Professor Raeder knew, unique; Sandra, nine, a telehypnotist of erratic brilliance.

"As I see it," said Professor Raeder, "the situation is of classic simplicity. It is a case of Mahomet and the mountain. We, collectively, are Mahomet, Vanessa Smith is the mountain. We must call her to come to us. We must use every means — persuasion, hypnotic suggestion, terror. We must build in her a compulsion to come to the Scottish Highlands. But, if that fails, we must be prepared to go to her. She is the burning glass we need. She is the one who can accept your transmissions and focus them into a tight beam. She is the one who will enable your combined talents to destroy this creature Humboldt. From now on, you will conduct an assault on Vanessa around the clock. It will be done in relays. Janine will weaken her — soften her up, I believe, is the phrase. Then Alfred will block undesirable contacts while Sandra and Robert combine to make her come to us. That there are flaws in this programme, I am aware. We do not know precisely where Vanessa is.

"We do not know this because she herself does not know it. But we do know that she has comfortable surroundings, that she is physically fit and that she feels secure. We know that she is in a country cottage and that she is being protected — if that is the right word — by an artist who calls himself Oliver Anderson. We have found all these things in Vanessa's mind."

"He hasn't screwed her," interrupted Janine. "I would have known if he had." She gave a twisted smile. "Even if I didn't have it with her at the time, I would have known."

"Dear Janine," said Professor Raeder in a deceptively gentle tone, "we are all painfully aware of your major interest in life. Please do not let it intrude upon rational discussion of a problem. Otherwise, I may be reluctantly compelled to apply electrodes to your temples."

Janine blanched at the threat. "I thought it was important," she said defensively. "If he screws her properly, she won't have any blocks left. Then we get a clear picture."

"Janine, the crudity of your expression is matched only by your inability to concentrate upon anything but personal gratification." The Professor's voice hardened. "You really will have to control yourself, my dear. I can assure you that the threat of electro-convulsive therapy is not an idle threat ... Now where was I?"

Sandra, munching peanuts, said helpfully: "Things we found in Vanessa's mind."

"Ah, yes. From the data you have supplied, my children, certain deductions may be made about this Mr. Anderson. We know he has some facial disfigurement. That knowledge is something Vanessa cannot cancel. We have also learned that, at the beginning, there was some confusion about his name and profession. Vanessa has constructed a deep block about this; and that, in itself, is interesting. Let us consider two hypothesis: one is that Mr. Anderson may be very intelligent, the other is that he may not be what he claims to be."

Alfred, smoking pot, was sufficiently with proceedings to say: "Suppositions aren't going to help us, Prof. We need the hard stuff."

Professor Raeder rubbed his hands together and smiled benevolently. "Are they not, Alfred, my boy? Are they not? Let us see. Let us try association of ideas. For example, what does the name Oliver suggest to you? Come on, tell me. No matter how ridiculous, tell me."

There was silence for a moment or two. Then Sandra, helping herself to more peanuts, said uncertainly: "Biscuits?"

Professor Raeder felt happy. For a short time he really could imagine himself back in tutorial with a handful of picked students. "Very good, Sandra. Bath Olivers are a kind of biscuit which I, personally, find very civilised ... Now, any other associations?"

Again there was a silence. Then Robert, who was not eating peanuts or smoking pot or dwelling upon orgasms

79

he had experienced vicariously, said with some hesitation: "Roland."

Professor Raeder seemed both surprised and delighted. "Ah, yes. Roland! Why did you say Roland, dear boy?"

Robert looked blank. "Don't know, Prof. It just seemed to come, that's all."

Raeder exuded triumph. None of the young paranormals could really understand his peculiar moods — which, perhaps, was one of the reasons he maintained his power over them. They knew he was exceptionally clever and somewhat vindictive. He had a great talent for dividing and conquering, also a talent for devising peculiarly apt punishments.

Janine tried a gentle flash probe, and was instantly rewarded with a mental picture of herself, unconscious, jerking horrifically under the stimulus of electro-convulsive therapy. She turned pale.

"Don't try that again, Janine," the Professor said softly. "You have been repeatedly warned of the penalties for attempting to invade my privacy. You are courting disaster."

"I'm sorry, sir," she said meekly. "I wasn't thinking."

"Maintain that condition, by all means," he responded icily. "I am here to do your thinking for you. But never, *never* disobey. That is my final warning . . ." He turned to the others. "Now why should Oliver be associated with Roland?"

No one knew. Robert felt he ought to know; but he didn't. Surreptitiously, he began to masturbate, out of sheer anxiety.

"Charlemagne," said Professor Raeder, "was king of the Franks about twelve centuries ago. He had two great knights, or generals, equally matched in fighting strength. One was called Oliver, and the other — "

"Roland" said Quasimodo helpfully.

"Exactly. Let us suppose that this man Oliver Anderson — about whose identity Vanessa seems to have voluntarily or involuntarily created a deep block — is not really Oliver Anderson. Let us suppose also that he, like the rest of us mere mortals, is subject to the process known as association of ideas. If, in a stress situation, he had to quickly invent a new persona and, more important, a new name for himself, might he not choose something remotely connected with his real name?"

"But if he did, if his real name is Roland, how can that help us?" Alfred was as puzzled as the rest of the group.

"Ah!" Professor Raeder rubbed his hands together. "What else do we know about this mysterious Oliver who might or might not be a Roland?"

"There is something wrong with his face."

"Yes, indeed. There is something wrong with his face. And that, my children, leads me to the not unreasonable conclusion that the man who is sheltering Vanessa Smith is Dr. Roland Badel, a psychologist who, I recall, was once attacked by a psychotic patient and badly disfigured. We will conduct our telepathic assault upon Vanessa; but if that fails, we shall begin to look for Dr. Roland Badel."

12

It was a fine morning. Vanessa was out walking in the woods, taking some pleasure in the sunshine and trying to forget the terrors of the night. Oliver had showed her the places where she could go in comparative safety. His house was more than a mile from the next one, and that was only occupied by an elderly forester employed by the National Parks Commission.

The valley in which Oliver Anderson lived was, so he assured Vanessa, well off the beaten track. Occasionally, tourists could be expected; but the whine of their hovercars gave ample warning of their arrival. Unless someone actually knew where Vanessa was, the chances of her being discovered by accident were remote.

Vanessa was walking upon a carpet of bluebells, inhaling their scent gratefully, using it and the shafts of sunlight that penetrated the densely-packed trees to exorcise the phantoms of darkness. Oliver had gone into the nearest town to get supplies of food and to buy a portable tri-di. Now that he had Vanessa to look after, he felt he needed once more to know what was going on in the outside world.

It had been an exhausting night. After a couple of hours of listening to music, which, besides giving pleasure, allowed her to relax her blocks, Vanessa had gone to bed early. She slept in a little attic room at the top of the house, directly above Oliver's bedroom.

She had tried very hard to sleep. But, it seemed, the moment she closed her eyes and relaxed, she had been invaded.

The invaders did not produce patterns she recognised. They were cold, demented patterns of thought, full of pressure, full of threat. They were like malignant worms, crawling into her, eating up her personality, implanting strange notions.

One of them whispered: 'I am Janine, you soft bitch. I know you. I can become you if I wish. You can fight against me, but in the end you will do what I want you to do... Leave him, Vanessa, leave him. He will betray you. We love you, we need you, we will never betray you.'

Another said: 'I can make you kill yourself, Vanessa. I can kill rats by willing them to die. I can kill you. It will take longer, but I can kill you.'

After that, there were images of mountains, blue skies and tranquil lakes. Images of peace and security. They made Vanessa feel that if only she could find such mountains and lakes all her troubles would be ended. She did not know whether such visions were of her own creation, or whether they had been created by the intruders.

Then came more whisperings, insidious, threatening.

'Join us, Vanessa, or we will come for you. Join us or we will destroy you. We know about you, Vanessa. We know all about you.'

Then came images of death — a coffin, a wreath of flowers, a skull grinning vacantly, a half-rotted corpse, a headless girl lying naked on a hillside, incredibly mutilated and with blood pouring from her dreadful wounds.

Vanessa made no response to these unknown, sinister

invaders. She tried blocks. They were, perhaps, sufficient to maintain the privacy of her own deepest thoughts and feelings; but they were not strong enough to reject the obscene images. Her mind was as outraged as if her body had been gripped and pinched and hurt by cruel fingers.

Again there were images of serenity. Pine forest, lakes, mountains, an old house that seemed remote from all the cares and troubles of the world. Remote from all nightmares . . .

And the voices once more.

'We'll always be with you, Vanessa. You can't escape us.'

'Dear Vanessa, you are so open. I can kill you, I think.'

'Why hasn't he screwed you yet, you soft, weak bitch? Are you so ugly?'

'Vanessa, you are going to die. Some day soon, unless you join us, you are going to die. It will be lovely. I haven't killed a girl before.'

'GO AWAY! GET OUT, YOU COLD FILTHY SHAPES. GO AWAY! OR I WILL FOLLOW AND BURN YOUR MINDS!'

It was loud.

It was strong.

It was terrifically strong.

It wasn't Vanessa.

But she knew who it was. Joyfully, she knew.

'Dugal!'

'Vanessa!' Thought patterns flowed together in affection, relief, recognition.

'Your shape is so strong, Dugal. What has happened? You never had this strength before.' She had felt the impact of his blast on the invaders. It must have deafened them. It had routed them, sent them crawling worm-like out of her mind.

'Lindemann gave me a shot. He said it would help me do anything I want to do. It has, hasn't it? Even you can't hope to block me now — with music or poetry or anything. I can go anywhere in your thoughts, dear Vanessa. But I won't do anything to hurt you. I promise.'

Suddenly, Vanessa was filled with dread, and dread accentuated by the knowledge that Dugal would instantly sense it.

'Lindemann? Oh!'

'What's wrong, Vanessa? Dr. Lindemann is a friend, isn't he? He wants to know if you are safe. He wants to know where you are, who you are with.'

'Dugal, forgive me. You are very young, very trusting. I want to be free, but Lindemann wants me back in prison, or worse.'

'You are sure?'

'Yes, I am sure.'

There was a pause. She felt his perplexity.

'WOULD HE LIE TO ME, VANESSA?'

'Dugal, please. Your probing hurts.'

'I'm sorry. Would he lie to me, Vanessa? How's that?'

'Better. Much better. Yes, he would lie to you, Dugal. He would lie to anyone, if it suited his purpose.'

'Oh . . . I love you, Vanessa. I always have. You are my true sister. I never had a sister. I don't even know who my parents were. But you are my true sister.'

'You are my true brother, Dugal. And I love you also.'

'Will you open to me?'

'Dugal, love, you are so young.'

'Will you open to me? I can go as deep as I wish,

85

but will you open to me? ... I'm not quite as young as you think ... I didn't know Dr. Lindemann was bad, Vanessa. But if you say he is, I believe you. I won't tell him anything you don't want me to tell him. I promise ... It's funny. He is one of the few people I can never flash-probe.'

'I think that is because he has an interrupter implanted in his skull, Dugal. You can see a scar when he bends his head.'

'What is an interrupter?'

'I don't truly know. Some kind of electronic gadget, I think. It insulates the thinking processes from outside interference. But it doesn't ensure privacy — except from paranormals like us. Somebody, somewhere, can probe Dr. Lindemann electronically as we can probe normals telepathically.'

'Will you open to me, Vanessa?'

She gave what amounted to a telepathic shrug. 'Do I need to? You have shown me your strength, Dugal. I cannot stop you.'

Dugal revealed anguish. 'You are my sister. I won't hurt you. But I need to know you. I can't bear to be cut off.'

Vanessa resigned herself. 'Then I will open, Dugal. For you only. Do not give my secrets to Lindemann. That would bring disaster.'

'I promise. I truly promise.'

Vanessa, lying in the dark, let all her mental tautness go. Dugal, after all, was the only kind of brother she would ever have. There had to be someone you could trust completely, if only a child ...

He was gentle. He did not hurt or press. He was gentle and loving, finding his way through her thoughts with childlike wonder. It did not take long. It does not take long to see all the elements in a picture hanging on a wall. But it does take time to appreciate the subtlety of their arrangement, the balance of interdependence ... It was, for Dugal, like looking at a very private picture in a private gallery.

'You love this man, this Roland Badel who protects you by being Oliver Anderson. I see he is old and his face is frightening. But you love him.' A statement, not a question. Dugal had seen it in the picture.

Vanessa had not seen it. She was confused. 'I don't know. Perhaps. I must think of him only as Oliver. So must you. Help me.'

'Dear Vanessa, I will help you. I don't mind that you love him. I will try to love him also ... Why don't you know where you are?'

'Oliver thinks it better that I don't ... The shapes you drove away, they want to find out.'

'Who are they? Do you know them?'

She shuddered. 'I know only that they are horrible. They are full of death and hate ... What will you tell Lindemann?'

'What do you want me to tell him?'

'Tell him — tell him I am somewhere in Scotland.' Vanessa did not know why she chose Scotland. 'Tell him I have joined a group of escaped paranormal children ... Tell him anything, Dugal, but the truth. And, Dugal, when you go, don't come back to me. It is too dangerous. One day we shall be happy together, but not yet.'

In her mind, she made an image of a long golden seashore. She and Dugal were walking along it, picking up sea-shells, throwing smooth flat pebbles at the sea, trying to make the pebbles bounce upon its surface.

Dugal entered the spirit of the dream. He invented a great pebble, smooth as a discus, and flung it out to sea. It bounced and bounced and went on skimming towards the horizon.

They both stood and watched it, hand in hand, watching in wonder.

'Vanessa, the pebble will go on bouncing across the water until it comes to another country. We are riding upon it. In that other country we shall be safe.'

'Yes, Dugal. We shall be safe.' Vanessa dissolved the vision because it made her want to cry. 'Don't forget that Lindemann is our enemy.'

'I won't forget. I'll leave you now. You are very tired.'

'Yes, I am tired. I want to rest so much.'

But Dugal came back later in the night. He came back because he must have been keeping guard, watching, waiting. He came back when the evil shapes invaded her head once more, trying to terrify her into submission.

He came back with such a fierce blast of energy that, hundreds of miles away, Quasimodo went into shock and complained of fires burning in his mind, while Janine writhed with pain and stared in wonder at blisters that were forming on her hands. Professor Raeder inspected them and knew what they were. As a parapsychologist he was familiar with stigmata. The stigmata of the damned.

For two or three hours before daybreak, Vanessa managed to get some sleep; but it was restless and dream-laden. Not all the dreams were bad. She dreamed of a misshapen boy, a stranger, yet a known stranger, whose mind was full of hate. But she also dreamed of summer days, of great stretches of waters, smooth as glass and, like glass, mirroring perfectly the great mountains that rose around them. And she dreamed of whispering forests and of a time when she and Oliver and Dugal were together in eternal sunshine.

Now, as she walked upon the carpet of bluebells, stretching like a brilliant faerie haze through the quiet sun-shifted woodlands, she tried to relax; but suddenly her mind was imbued with a nameless indefinable terror.

She recognised the symptom. Somehow, she had achieved an involuntary rapport with someone under immense stress. She felt beads of sweat forming on her forehead. She felt her hands shaking. She felt her heart pounding.

And suddenly she was no longer in a faerie haze of bluebells. She was at Random Hill with Dugal.

She was in a lavatory.

'I tried not to call you, Vanessa. I tried . . . I tried!' He was crying, shaking, full of fear.

Through his eyes, Vanessa saw the tiles, the lavatory seat on which he was standing, the door. She saw the cistern above his head, the tie that he had fastened to it. The other end was looped round his neck with a slip-knot. She felt the loop upon his throat.

'Hush, Dugal. You didn't call. I came to you. What is it? What's happening?'

'Lindemann. He didn't believe what I told him . . . Vanessa, I'm sorry. I'm not much good at lying. He didn't believe about Scotland and the paras. He's going to shoot me full of something that will make me tell the truth whether I want to or not.'

She tried to soothe him. 'That's all right, Dugal. It was bound to happen. Don't cry, little brother. It was bound to happen. I can take care of myself.'

'Vanessa, I promised you!'

'Hush, it doesn't matter.'

'It does! It does! Because I love you and I will not

break the promise ... I asked him if I could go to the lavatory before he gave me the shot. There isn't much time Vanessa, my sister. Say you love me. Say it again. Say that one day we shall look for sea-shells together.'

'Dugal, darling, you are not to do it!'

'Say it, Vanessa. SAY IT!'

'Dugal, I love you truly. You are my beloved brother. We shall look for sea-shells together ... Please, Dugal, please, my darling brother, don't do it.'

'I love you. I am only a child, but I love you. And even a child can die for the one he loves. Remember the sea-shells.'

'Dugal, don't! Don't do it!'

Vanessa was too late. There were knocks on the lavatory door. She heard Dr. Lindemann's voice.

Then Dugal jumped from the lavatory seat.

She felt the tie suddenly biting into his neck. She felt the brilliant flash of light as his spinal cord was broken. She felt darkness engulf Dugal, and engulf her also.

Then she fell unconscious upon a carpet of bluebells.

13

DR. LINDEMANN FINALLY managed to batter the door open. Dugal his head twisted at an unnatural angle and his face distorted, was hanging with his feet almost touching the floor. The stainless steel pipe from which he had hanged himself was considerably bent. Dr. Lindemann wished vainly that it had fractured before Dugal's neck was broken. A glance told him that there was no hope of resuscitation. The body, pathetic and terrible, swung slowly, the limp arms moving with a grotesque illusion of life.

Dr. Lindemann, less concerned with the death of a child than with his own problems, contemplated his immediate future. It seemed bleak.

Later, he tried to justify himself to Professor Holroyd, head of Random Hill. Professor Holroyd, white-haired, near to retirement, had never liked Lindemann, had never approved of his methods. Holroyd was a humanist, Lindemann was a pragmatist — a career scientist who would sacrifice anything, including people, to further his own aims. For some time, Lindemann had been regarded by almost everyone except Professor Holroyd as a golden boy — because he produced results. But now his crash-training techniques for paranormal children had come unstuck.

The interview took place within minutes of Dugal's

death. Dr. Lindemann, Profesor Holroyd noted with some satisfaction, was still in a state of shock.

"It looks bad, Lindemann. It looks very bad. But I will do what I can for you. It may not be much ... After all, one of your group has absconded and another has committed suicide. There is bound to be an inquiry — particularly since Vanessa Smith has become a political pawn ... Do you know why this child — what is he called — Dugal — hanged himself?"

"Sir," said Dr. Lindemann desperately, "I can only conclude that he was unstable."

"So. You did not know that he was unstable?"

"No, sir."

"Then you are incompetent, Dr. Lindemann. You are not fit to be entrusted with the training and development of gifted children."

"It was a very difficult situation, Professor Holroyd. The security people have been pressing very hard — about Vanessa. The boy Dugal was my best chance of learning what has happened to her. There was a rapport relationship between them."

"So. The boy Dugal is dead. I do not think he killed himself because he was bored. Why did he kill himself, Dr. Lindemann? What pressure did you apply?"

"Professor Holroyd, I have done nothing that cannot be justified. I gave Dugal Amplia Nine so that he could read Vanessa Smith with or without her consent. Afterwards, I realised that he would not voluntarily tell me all he had learned, so I prepared to give him an injection of Veranon."

"You told him what you were doing?""

"Yes, sir. I did not want to have to use the truth drug. I thought the threat would be sufficient. After all, he was only a child."

"Yes," said Professor Holroyd heavily, "he was only

a child ... But some children have clearer vision than adults, Dr. Lindemann. It is obvious that Dugal did not wish to be chemically violated. His relationship with Vanessa was, evidently, stronger than you supposed. So he chose to preserve his freedom in his own fashion ... Later, I will drink to that. Meanwhile, we have you to consider."

"Yes, sir," said Dr. Lindemann hopefully. "What would you recommend?"

Professor Holroyd gave him a distant smile. "I would recommend that you make sure your passport is in order. His Majesty's loyal Opposition already know about Vanessa, and seek to embarrass the government. The affair is now of some magnitude. No doubt the leader of the New Consensus Party will learn presently of the death of Dugal Nemo from the same source that revealed the disappearance of Vanessa Smith. I think that will surely harden parliamentary resistance to the Security of the State Bill — to Sir Joseph's acute political embarrassment. The Prime Minister does not like to be embarrassed; and you, Lindemann, have become a great source of embarrassment ... Yes, if I were you, I should be thinking in terms of foreign travel. Extensive travel. I am told it broadens the mind."

Sweat formed on Lindemann's forehead. "I can't understand how the news of Vanessa leaked," he said desperately. "Unless there is a para spy here at Random Hill, and that is plainly impossible. So how could they learn of Dugal's death unless — " he stopped.

Professor Holroyd was enjoying himself. "Exactly. Unless someone in authority told them."

"You!"

"Dr. Lindemann, there are still a number of people who are old-fashioned enough to believe that human beings should be treated as human beings. That is one of the reasons I accepted my present appointment — so that I could act as a brake upon people like you, power-hungry career men backed by Humboldt's dogs. You are not a scientist. You are not even much of a human being. You are just a little man on the make. Well, you have gambled, Lindemann, and you have lost."

"You!" Lindemann reached for the V-phone.

Holroyd shrugged. "Use it by all means, dear fellow. Your star sender escaped, your star probe committed suicide. And now you are about to accuse me of professional indiscretion. Use the V-phone if you wish. It is the surest way of bringing Humboldt's dogs upon you."

Lindemann collapsed, a shaking wreck. "What shall I do? What shall I do?"

"See that your passport is in order," said Holroyd patiently. "Move fast. Do not stay in one place over long." He smiled. "You might offer your services and experiences in Eastern Europe. If they accepted you, that would be the safest course of all."

"I am not a criminal or a traitor. I don't want to run."

"There is an alternative," suggested Professor Holroyd with some malice. "The one that Dugal Nemo took."

Jenny Pargetter was drained — physically, emotionally, intellectually. The paranormals of the Department of Internal Security had probed her mind with professional thoroughness, carefully examining all the images, memories and associations they found.

Jenny had felt them, had felt an invasion she was powerless to stop, had felt a succession of cold, almost impersonal phantoms plucking at her most private thoughts, looking coolly at her most cherished memories. She shuddered each time she remembered the process. Once or twice it had made her physically sick. It was like being raped successively by strangers who did not even take pleasure in their violence.

She was sitting in the small but comfortably furnished room that had been placed at her disposal. It was in what, apparently, had once been a secluded country house, far enough away from London to give a sense of isolation. She did not know where Simon was; but she had been allowed to talk to him by V-phone less than half an hour ago. He had not looked very happy. Presumably, he, too, had been probed. Presumably, he, too, felt wretched.

The last interrogator had told her that her ordeal was over. In a tightly controlled voice she had asked when she would be released and reunited with her husband. The interrogator had not answered her question. He had made polite, sympathetic noises and told her to relax, indicating the drinks and cigarettes on a sideboard, the tri-di, the stereo player, the tape library, the books on the shelves. He told her that Denzil Ingram would be along presently; and meanwhile the best thing to do was try to forget all the regrettable but necessary things that had happened.

Then, very quickly, he had left the room. It was then that Jenny noticed that there was no handle on the door. She wondered how the interrogator had opened it.

According to her watch, the interrogator had been gone just over twenty minutes. During that time, Jenny had smoked three cigarettes and had drunk about a quarter of a bottle of neat Scotch whisky. It was a very good whisky; but apart from making her feel slightly warmer, it seemed to have little effect.

She was just pouring herself another drink when Denzil Ingram entered the room noiselessly. She was so surprised to see him as she turned that she almost dropped her glass of whisky.

"Forgive me, Mrs. Pargetter. I didn't mean to startle you."

"I suppose creeping comes naturally to one in your profession."

He refused to take offence. "May I sit down?"

Jenny had heard her voice rising and made an effort to control it. "This is your territory, Mr. Ingram. You have already demonstrated that you do not need my permission to do anything."

He smiled. "Then I, too, will drink some of the state's whisky." Ingram poured himself a generous measure. "Let us relax and have a talk."

"As you can see," she said bitterly, "I am in no mood to relax. Nor do I want to have a talk. I just want to get away from this place with my husband as fast as possible."

"All in good time," he soothed. "Believe me, Mrs. Pargetter, I want to make things easy for you. I know what being probed is like." He took a drink and smiled at her. "Every time I was promoted, I had to undergo total probe. I have been completely 'washed out', as we say, three times." He stared at her intently. "It's a rape of the mind, you know. We live in cruel times."

"If that is how you feel, why do you allow it to be done to innocent people such as me and my husband?"

He shrugged. "Necessity. I have a job to do. Sometimes I like it, sometimes I don't. This time I don't.'"

"Necessity! Everything from blackmail to murder can be justified under that heading."

"True," he said calmly, "but my concern is the safety of the realm. And I will employ any method that enables me to discharge my duty."

"At least you are honest." Jenny swallowed her whisky, and began to feel a reluctant admiration for Denzil Ingram.

"I try to be. If I am dishonest, it is not because I want to be ... Now, Mrs. Pargetter, I will be completely honest with you. Oddly, I like you — and that is why I am prepared to declare all my options. But first let us talk about Vanessa."

Jenny poured herself another drink. Ingram raised an eyebrow, but made no comment.

"Yes, let us talk about Vanessa. Your minions screwed my mind until I had to vomit."

"I know and I am sorry."

"Your sorrow is noted. So let us talk about Vanessa."

"You were very helpful. We now know who is protecting her."

Jenny was amazed. "I didn't know, so how could you — ?"

"It's easy, The white man's magic. Computers. You gave us the vital clue. A picture of a man whose face had been badly injured. We turned that over to the computer network. It has access to all hospital records for the last twenty years. Amazingly, there turned out to be nearly thirty thousand people with severe facial injuries. But roughly half these were women. The picture we got from you was of a man who had suffered recent injuries. We were able to narrow the field to four thousand cases. The picture suggested an age range of thirty-five to forty-five. We narrowed to one thousand eight hundred. His hair was dark, and he had an educated voice. We cut down to four hundred and eighty-one males. He lived in seclusion in a rural area. That reduced us to one hundred and twelve possibles ... You were born in the South Downs, weren't you, Mrs. Pargetter?"

"Yes." Jenny held her glass of whisky tensely, not drinking it. "But what has that to do with it?"

"You recognised some of the country Vanessa had

seen on her flight from Random Hill. That reduced our field to seventeen possibles. My men have been busy. Eight possibles have been eliminated. That leaves nine who cannot at present be traced. Out of those nine, the computer has selected a maximum probability. His name is Roland Badel, doctor of psychology. He is the one. Somewhere in the South Downs, he is sheltering Vanessa."

"Assuming your computer to be infallible — which I doubt — how does all this effect me and my husband?"

Denzil Ingram sighed. Now came the hard part. He wasn't betting either way. Women were the damnedest creatures. But sometimes they could be practical. Sometimes.

"Mrs. Pargetter, let us be frank with each other. It's the only way we can arrive at an understanding. If I were to release you and your husband now, what would you do?"

She gave a bitter laugh. "Have me probed and find out."

"I could do, but I don't want to. Unnecessary brutality is abhorrent to me . . . Nor is it elegant to crack a walnut with a sledgehammer."

"Elegant! That is a nice choice of word . . . So you consider me as a walnut ready for the cracking?"

"Forgive me. It was a bad metaphor. But you must bear in mind that I am empowered to use the metaphorical sledgehammer. It is vitally important for you to remember that. Now, please tell me honestly what you would do, and I will be equally honest with you."

"Mr. Ingram, you continue to amaze me. You are the most polite thug I have ever encountered." Oddly, Jenny felt less tense. There was obviously going to be some kind of showdown and, in a way, she felt relieved.

Ingram helped himself to more whisky. "I fear your

experience of thugs is limited, Mrs. Pargetter. But please answer my question. It is important."

Jenny took a deep breath. "Well, then, I shall talk to the newspapers. I shall tell them all that has happened — and I shall add the information you have just given me that Vanessa is alive and well. And how do you like that, Mr. Ingram?"

He smiled. "I like your honesty. The newspapers I can fix, of course. They won't print a word of what you say."

"Then, if necessary, I'll stand on a soap-box at Speakers' Corner. There is still some freedom left in this country."

"I am sorry to disillusion you, but freedom is already a casualty of the age ... But to return to matters practical. Vanessa has become of political significance, Mrs. Pargetter. If I could have found her shortly after her escape, all would have been well, relatively speaking. But now it is politically necessary that she does not exist. We have a problem."

"You have a problem," flashed Jenny. "My course of action is crystal clear."

"No, Mrs. Pargetter. *You* have a problem. Because, you see, I am in control of events."

"What do you mean?" Jenny was trembling. She hoped it was not visible, but she knew it was.

"You have been honest. I will honour my bargain. I have several options. If necessary — and I hope it won't be — I can have you and your husband killed. It would, of course, look like an accident. Let us say a hovercar accident. Or it could even look like a suicide pact, with explanatory notes left which the experts would undoubtedly testify to be authentic. All this would depend on departmental strategy. I mention these distasteful possibilities only to emphasise the seriousness of the situation."

Jenny was visibly going to pieces. She helped herself to more whisky, slopping as much around the glass as she managed to pour into it.

"I see," she said in an unnaturally calm voice. "You are offering a bargain. My life and my husband's life for Vanessa's life. You want to kill her and you want us to remain silent."

"Not as bad as that," he lied. "I want your silence in exchange for keeping Vanessa out of the political arena. I want to hide her away until this whole affair has died down."

"And until Black Joe gets what he wants and feels secure?"

"You could put it like that."

"I do ... How can I be sure that you will not kill Vanessa, anyway?"

"I could arrange for you to write to Vanessa and she to you."

Jenny stifled a sob. "I don't even know her handwriting. You could get anyone to write the letters."

"You can have photographs also."

Jenny threw her whisky glass against the wall. "Your rapists have done their work. You must know that I have no idea what she looks like!"

"Then I will even arrange for you to meet her regularly." Ingram remained calm, damnably calm.

"But I still won't know her," said Jenny desperately, "because I never did know her. You would be able to pass off any obliging little zombie as Vanessa."

Denzil Ingram played his ace. "If you are as tele-pathically close to her as our investigations suggest, you will know her. You will find a way of knowing her. If

100

there is any doubt, you can have her independently probed."

"I see. Give me some whisky, please. I'm sorry I'm making a scene. I hate scenes. But then it is not every day that one is coolly threatened with murder... In any case, even if I agreed to remain silent, how could you be sure I would keep my promise?"

Ingram gave her the whisky. "I have the necessary insurance, Mrs Pargetter. If you were so foolish as to try to prove that Vanessa exists, she would have to die. Already, as you know, contingency plans have required us to destroy all known records. There is now no record of Vanessa's' birth. Her data has been expunged from all relevant computer storage systems. Legally, and for all practical purposes, she is now a girl who never was. It is easy to dispose of someone who does not exist. You take my point?"

"I take your point, damn you. But what of the time when Vanessa is no longer of political significance? Will you let her go?"

"Yes, but she will have to have a new identity. There should be no difficulty about that."

"Then I accept your bargain, Mr. Ingram. I loathe it, and I loathe myself. But I want Vanessa to live, and so I accept."

"That is very wise, Mrs. Pargetter. Very sensible. I am so sorry you have had such a rough time. You and your husband will be able to leave shortly. Naturally, you will be under some kind of surveillance for a while; but you will never notice it, I assure you."

"And Vanessa?"

"Don't worry about Vanessa. We shall pick her up and look after her very carefully. She will be treated well. You will see her soon, then you can judge for yourself."

Denzil Ingram sounded utterly sincere. That was one of his great strengths. He could always make himself sound utterly sincere.

There was no indication that he had already mentally signed death warrants for Jenny and Simon Pargetter. All he needed was a little time — enough time to take Vanessa out. Jenny Pargetter would give him that time because she believed him. And when Vanessa was dead, all would be well. The Pargetters could meet with a sad accident — with plenty of irreproachable witnesses — and then the case of Vanessa Smith would be closed for ever.

Professor Raeder had gathered his little group together for a final briefing. He looked at them carefully. They did not look very formidable. In fact they looked ridiculously young, ridiculously stupid, ridiculously ineffectual and — in the case of Quasimodo — somewhat grotesque. But he also saw them as something else: as components of a great psychological machine of destruction; a machine that would destroy the government of the United Kingdom and give Professor Raeder the power he had craved for so long. There remained the problem of the missing component — the vital mechanism that would bring the machine to life. It would have to be obtained quickly.

"So, my children, our campaign of terror has not yet yielded results. I do not entirely blame you, though I must confess to some disappointment. The interference did not help, of course. It came at a time when Vanessa lacked confidence in her powers to reject. Alas, it also reinforced her, renewed her determination to resist our onslaught."

He smiled benevolently. "Judging from the immediate effects on Quasimodo and Janine — which, I am happy to say, produced no permanent damage — the sender was emitting signals of quite exceptional strength. This leads me to conclude either that he possessed paranormal resources of unprecedented power, or that he had used one of the few booster drugs, possibly Amplia Nine. The latter is more probable. In which case, our interfering friend will live to regret his extravagance. However, this is beside the point.

"Time, my young friends, is our enemy. Vanessa will not come to us. Therefore we must go to Vanessa. I will take Quasimodo and Janine. The rest of you will stay here. As we travel south, we shall take fixes. Telefixes are difficult but not impossible. I think we shall be able to ascertain where Vanessa is hiding. We already have impressions of hills and woodland and luxuriant countryside. A sea of bluebells was the last reported visual. I think it is important. Also, I have been able to chart Vanessa's most probable route from Random Hill."

Professor Raeder paused. "To those of you who remain here, let me give a final word of warning. Do not try to escape. Being a person of some foresight, as you know, I have surrounded this house with buried proximity mines which can be activated or de-activated electronically. When I and Quasimodo and Janine take the hovercar south, I shall activate the mines. I would not recommend any of you to try to walk more than twenty metres from the house . . . You have ample stores of food, and I do not expect we shall be away very long. Alfred, you are in charge and accountable. You know how our defence system works; but you are not to use it without first consulting me through Janine or Quasimodo. One or the other will remain open to you most of the time. Incidentally, I will make routine contact with you once every three hours.

103

"I ask no more than that you should behave sensibly for two, perhaps three days. Is that too much to ask?"

"No, sir," said Alfred dutifully.

"So," said Professor Raeder cheerfully. "We will now proceed to acquire our burning glass."

14

THE MAN WHO had conditioned himself to become Oliver Anderson had driven back to his secluded cottage with a strange and satisfying sense of homecoming. The house had never felt like a home before. But now it did; and that was entirely due to the presence of Vanessa. She was the first person he had met about whom he cared not professionally but personally, deeply personally. He told himself that the age gap was too great. They were separated by nearly twenty years. It did not seem to matter.

Did he regard her as a woman whom he might bed or as a child whom he might cherish? He did not know. He chose not to know. The disturbing fact of love was sufficient unto itself.

It was late morning when he got back to the cottage. The tri-di he had bought was a small portable model with a built-in permanent atomic power source. The holopix it displayed lacked the high definition of a lounge tri-di; but that did not matter. The tri-di was simply a necessary window through which could be observed some, at least, of the discreetly exposed machinations of Sir Joseph Humboldt.

Oliver had also bought a great deal of food not because he was anticipating any kind of siege or difficulty in obtaining further supplies but because he wished to leave Vanessa alone as little as possible.

He was not greatly surprised by her absence upon his return. The sky was blue, the sun was bright, the air was warm. He was glad that she was out in the woods enjoying an almost perfect spring day. She had told him of her terrifying experiences during the night, and he had chided her, gently, for not calling him. He had made her promise that, if there were any further nocturnal invasions, she would tell him immediately. His professional mind — still active and acute, despite his assumption of a new role — told him that the invaders wanted to possess Vanessa, wanted to use her for some purpose yet to be revealed. He was filled with apprehension at their persistence and at the methods they used. But he was also partly reassured by the fact that they could not know where she was, simply because Vanessa did not know where she was.

She had told him also about Dugal's intervention. He was glad that she had a friend, even if only a small boy. But he was filled with anxiety that she had freely opened to Dugal. Even if the boy was absolutely loyal, it was placing too much responsibility upon him. But, then, the strength of his signals apparently was such that even if Vanessa had not opened, he could have pushed through her blocks and learned whatever he wanted to learn. According to Vanessa, Dugal had never been able to send so powerfully before. He had told her he had been given a shot — which pointed to a booster drug, possibly Amplia Nine. And if that were the case, how long would the child Dugal be able to hold out against those who were using him so unscrupulously to obtain information? Not long, decided the professional ghost who lived inside Oliver Anderson. They would know if he was holding back, and they

106

would simply stick a needle into his arm. Then, in a very short time, Humboldt's minions would be thoroughly acquainted with the eccentricities of one Roland Badel.

He looked at the groceries he had bought. They were superfluous, he realised. He should have thought the situation out hours ago — and made positive plans. One thing was clear. He and Vanessa would have to start moving — and keep on the move until the crisis was over. Until no one was interested any longer in the fate of Vanessa Smith. Tomorrow, he decided, they would begin to travel. Vanessa had talked wistfully of calm stretches of water, of mountains and forests of pine trees. Such things could be found in Scotland. Perhaps it would be a good idea to get lost in the North West Highlands . . .

Methodically, he unpacked the groceries and put them away, the perishables in the fridge, the irradiated fresh food on the cold slab in the larder. It was something to do. Something to do until Vanessa returned. When she came back, he would have a serious talk with her. They would face possibilities, probabilities, facts. He knew beyond any shadow of a doubt that he did not want to lose her, ever. A strange sensation for one who had been determined to reject the world and any emotional involvement with people. But a fact to be faced, along with the fact of Dugal and his vulnerability, along with the fact of the sinister unknowns who were fighting for possession of Vanessa's mind.

He looked at the clock, and was amazed to discover that the time was almost one-thirty. He had told Vanessa that he would return by one o'clock. She had agreed to be back by then. She wore a wristwatch. But the day was full of sunshine, full of warmth. No doubt she was entranced by the magical carpet of bluebells he had

107

shown her. Very likely she was absorbed in picking an armful to bring back to the house to fill it with their subtle but transient fragrance. He decided to go and look for her. He had shown her how far she could go. It would not take long to find her.

It did not take long to find her.

She was still lying where she had fallen among the bluebells; but she was no longer unconscious. Her body was shaken by a terrible and almost noiseless sobbing.

He knelt by her, gently lifted her shoulders, looked at her tear-stained face and held her head against his chest, stroking her hair.

"Vanessa, what is it? What's happened? Tell me about it, little one. Please tell me about it."

For a few seconds, she was unable to speak. Each time she opened her mouth, the tears welled from her eyes, her body shook and there was a great tightness in her throat — because she did not want to hear the words she would have to use. The words that would make Dugal's death a fact, a part of history.

Finally, she managed to control herself. Finally she managed to say: "Dugal is dead. Oh, Oliver, he killed himself for my sake. I was with him. I saw where he was. I felt him die. Poor Dugal ... Poor, trusting Dugal."

And then, somehow, she managed to tell what had happened. She told it coherently, almost unemotionally, as if she were relating a nightmare. Which, perhaps, it was. A nightmare tragedy in a nightmare world.

Oliver said nothing for a while. He just held her close, stroking her hair, thinking of the misery she had suffered and of the loneliness and the fear that had dominated so much of her young life.

At length he said softly: "I was afraid of Dugal. I was afraid of your relationship with him. I was afraid

108

he would betray you. I thought of him simply as a gifted but defenceless child. But now I, who was supposed to know about the workings of the mind, learn that a small boy may achieve the strength, the stature and the courage of a man — simply because he loves someone. I am humbled. I and my kind have been treating people as if they were no more than complicated machines. We have been trying to dehumanise the race of man. It seems now that we need to learn from those we have been trying to corrupt."

Vanessa managed a sad smile. "That is the voice of a ghost. The Oliver Anderson I know is only interested in painting, drinking and laying."

He seized gratefully upon her gentle reproof and attempted lightness. "You are right, love," he said, dropping into a northern accent, "I'm a dedicated man — and, like all great artists, essentially I'm a simple man. All I want to do is paint, booze and lay in peace and without interference from the bloody philistines. So, tomorrow, we'll move away from here. We'll lose ourselves properly. We'll find somewhere that's far away from all the cities. And then we'll take up the simple life for real — painting, boozing and laying." He helped her up. "Come on home, Vanessa. There is work to be done. Some packing and some thinking."

"Scotland?" suggested Vanessa. "I don't know why, but I have been thinking about Scotland quite a lot recently. It's ridiculous. I've never been there; but I feel I know the Highlands. There aren't many people there. I'd love to see the bare mountains and the deer forests and the glens and the lochs... Strange, isn't it?"

He shot her a curious glance. "Scotland is it, then? Well, I'm sorry about that, Vanessa. I was thinking of Cornwall or maybe Wales. Anyway, there's time enough to reach an amicable agreement before tomorrow."

Vanessa suddenly shivered, as if a chill wind was blowing. "I loved Dugal," she said. "I loved him very much."

Oliver took her hand in his. "And now I love him also, little one. He has bought some time for you. The price was high. Let us not abuse his gift. Tomorrow we will go to a place that is really safe. Do not ask me where it is."

Hand in hand, they walked across the carpet of bluebells, making their way back to the cottage, not knowing that tomorrow was already too late.

15

THE LAST NIGHT in the the cottage in the South Downs was one that Roland Badel would remember in great detail for the rest of his life. It was the first and last time that he and Vanessa went to bed together as man and woman. It was also the end of a brief idyll, the end of a poor charade.

They had gone to bed late, after carefully packing all the clothes and personal things they would need in the hovercar; and after Roland, still in his assumed role as Oliver Anderson, had selected paints, brushes, a couple of unfinished canvases and his easel. Then, for a while, he had drunk whisky and pored over maps.

He had also encouraged Vanessa to drink some whisky. She was still in a state of acute depression. She needed something to dull her misery and, perhaps, shut out the malign thought-invaders who seemed determined that she should get no rest at night.

In fact, that, rather than any overwhelming sexual compulsion was the reason he took her to share his bed. He wanted to reassure her with his physical presence. He wanted to put his arms round her, enfold her, tell her the unconvincing lie that there was nothing to fear.

Vanessa did not like the taste of whisky, even when it was mixed with water. She shuddered when she tasted it; but she drank it dutifully because Oliver said it would probably help.

She was half tipsy when they went to bed. The agonising experience of Dugal's death appeared at least to have been temporarily enshrouded in alcoholic mist. Besides being half tipsy, she was very tired.

He knew that she was a virgin. He knew that she was less than half his age. He knew that his real duty was to protect her and make her feel secure.

But when she lay beside him and snuggled close, none of that seemed quite so important as the living, exciting body that pressed against him.

He tried to sleep, tried to shut out all desire, all erotic thought. But Vanessa was restless; and her restlessness caused her to turn and sigh and moan. The invaders came with their sinister whisperings. They penetrated the mist and tried to hurt her. She pressed hard against him for comfort.

He tried to remain detached, tried to distract her, help her repel the intangible presences that seemed to have crept into the bed. But he found himself touching, stroking, caressing. He found himself kissing and holding with passion.

Sex, he rationalised wildly, was at least a kind of diversion. In the darkness he could visualise her wide open eyes, her open and responsive mouth.

Vanessa, her tension eased a little by the whisky, was amazed, excited, gratified by the strange sensations surging through her body. She felt with wonderment the liquid revelations of desire, the way her small breasts ached almost as if they were independent of her, the way her skin became supersensitive, somehow magnifying every touch and caress.

When she was a child, she remembered feeling snow flakes for the first time. The snow had seemed to chill her skin and at the same time bring it strangely alive. The snow flakes she felt now were not cold. Not cold at all. They were snow flakes of fire. But the fire warmed, gave life, rather than consumed.

Vanessa, at seventeen, was totally innocent. It was as if Nature had played a trick on her, had created a strange practical joke. On the one hand she possessed paranormal powers. Unlike ordinary human beings, her mind was not locked inside her head. It could receive messages directly from other minds. It could reach out. On the other hand, it seemed that Nature had compelled her to pay for this talent with physical retardation. Until the time when Roland Badel/Oliver Anderson held her close, she had never known desire.

Now, she discovered that it was a wondrous thing. She wanted time to savour it, to examine it. But the woman locked inside her knew that there was no time left at all.

In the darkness, Oliver said: "Perhaps I should not hold you like this. I am more than twice your age. I have known other women. You are still a virgin. Dear Vanessa, my only excuse is that I love you."

She stroked his shoulder. The skin felt soft and the muscles felt hard. There was strength and softness all mixed up together.

"My love, do what you want to do. That is what I want most of all. Already you make my body sing."

She hardly felt it when her hymen broke. She was too filled with wonder at the mysterious thing that leapt and pulsed inside her, making her body arch and throb with almost unendurable pleasure.

Vanessa, her mind and body intoxicated now with physical ecstasy as well as with a little whisky, did not even notice when the invader came, quietly exploring the labyrinth of her mind, probing, watching, gloating;

avidly absorbing all the sensual experience that came from the act of love.

But when it was all over, when Roland and Vanessa lay entwined with passion spent, Janine could not resist a telepathic shout of triumph.

'He screwed us well, didn't he, dear?' There was dreadful, silent laughter. 'What a pity he couldn't know he was having two trollops for the price of one!'

Vanessa cried out, shrank away from Roland, lay there shivering, feeling exposed, dirty, horrible. Trying desperately to drive the invader from her mind; but lacking the strength, the clarity and discipline to do so.

"What is it, love? What's happened? Did I hurt you?" Roland was perplexed. One moment Vanessa seemed on the edge of restful sleep, the next she was a shaking wreck.

She managed to speak calmly, "Someone has probed me. She's there still. She was there when — " Vanessa could not say it. For what had been wonderful was now humiliating and dirty.

Roland, now wide awake, tried to draw her close once more. "Don't panic, darling. Can you reject her? Can you get her out?"

"I'm trying," Vanessa said desperately. "I'm trying."

'Tell him I like his shoulders,' whispered Janine maliciously. 'Tell him I think he's got a big future — chiefly between his legs — for girls like you and me.'

Vanessa thrust away from Roland, and rolled to the edge of the bed, retching.

'Not much of a woman, are you, girlie?' whispered Janine. 'Never mind. I'll console him. I've got better tits than yours . . . We know where you are now, sweetie, and we're coming for you soon!'

Vanessa was physically sick. She began to vomit uncontrollably on to the bedroom floor. It was — though she did not know it — the best thing she could have done.

Janine could not endure the experience. She fled.

Roland Badel turned on the light and gazed in consternation and pity as Vanessa, who, not long ago had enjoyed the pleasures of love, now lay with her head over the side of the bed, her slender body racked by convulsions as she simultaneously wept and vomited.

"Turn off the light!" she managed to gasp. "I don't want you to see me like this."

He laid his hand gently on her back, stroked it, patted it as he would have stroked and patted a child. "I will not turn the light out," he said gently. "We will share suffering and humiliation as we share love."

Soon the horrible knotting and surging in her stomach was over. Vanessa lay on the bed helplessly, gasping for air, while tears fell from her eyes into the steaming vomit.

Now that she was over it, Roland went into action. Still naked, he dashed into the bathroom, found towels, brought them and cleaned up the helpless Vanessa. Finally, as she lay on the bed, he cleaned up the mess on the floor and sprayed the remaining damp patch liberally with an aerosol air-sweetener.

"She was inside me," said Vanessa dully, "feeling you as I felt you, watching, prying." She shuddered. "Even enjoying ... I can't think about it any more. I shall be sick again."

"Don't think about it, then," he said firmly. "Don't think about anything that has happened tonight. Think only that we are going away tomorrow — far, far away. And we are going to devise a way of getting rid of this kind of torment for good. I know a surgeon — a very good man — who has done a lot of work on paranormals with head injuries. When the furore has died down, I'll contact him. If I understood rightly, there is a fairly simple operation that will — "

"Oliver, please," she said faintly. "Not now. Tomorrow or the day after you shall tell me, but not now."

He cursed his stupidity. "I'm a fool. Forgive me." He gave a grim laugh. "I'm supposed to be the clever one. Forgive me. Tomorrow we will put a lot of miles behind us, and then — "

"Charming," said a male voice. "So informal, but quite charming. What is that dreadful smell?"

Roland whirled and saw a man standing in the doorway of the bedroom. "Who the devil are you? How did you get in? What do you want?"

"Rest easy, Dr. Badel. Don't try anything foolish."

"My name is Anderson."

"So?" The man in the doorway kept his hand in his pocket and advanced into the room. "Then I am one of the Brothers Grimm." He permitted himself the ghost of a smile. Then he frowned and looked disapprovingly at Vanessa. "You shouldn't have done that, my dear. A little knowledge is a dangerous thing."

Vanessa sat up on the bed, her small breasts firm and compactly beautiful, her hair matted about her shoulders, her eyes dark with fatigue, her face stained with recent anguish.

She looked at Roland and said unemotionally: "His name is Denzil Ingram. He is a government man and he has a laser pistol in his pocket. He came here to kill us."

16

INGRAM SAID: "I'm truly sorry you did that, Vanessa. You should not have been able to do it. But, then, I am told you have exceptional powers."

Now that he had at last found his prey, Ingram discovered with great annoyance that, for perhaps the first time in his professional career, he utterly loathed his task. He was a highly trained hunter, an expert in sudden death. In the course of his duties, he had been required to kill many people — spies, saboteurs, revolutionaries, would-be assassins. He had never enjoyed killing. It was like destroying a still functioning machine — like sending a perfectly good hovercar to the scrapyard.

But, formerly, killing could be justified by logic. It was necessary to take out spies, assassins and the like. He was paid and empowered to protect the security of the state. A grown man — or woman — who chose to attempt to disrupt the status quo was fully aware of the price of failure and therefore must be prepared to pay when the reckoning was presented.

But Vanessa Smith was not a revolutionary or an assassin. She was still only a child. All she had done was to escape from a school for paranormals. It was her tragedy that the Opposition was using her existence for political ends. It was her tragedy that Sir Joseph Humboldt needed her non-existence also for political ends. As far as the politicians were concerned, she was not a person — just an explosive Parliamentary Question.

And yet she was only a child — no, half a child and half a woman — sitting pathetically naked on a bed where she had doubtless learned about sex for the first and, sadly, the last time.

Strange how vulnerable people seemed when they were naked. She and Badel seemed frozen by shock. Denzil Ingram hoped very much that they had enjoyed what had evidently just passed between them. Otherwise, it would be doubly terrible to die in such circumstances. But must they die? He needed time to think.

"Put on your clothes," he said irritably. "You are sorry I'm here, and I am sorry I'm here. Put on your clothes, and we will all try to be civilised. But don't do anything stupid, Dr. Badel. I am trained for this sort of thing: you are not."

"I imagine," said Roland, "that it will be easier for you to kill us when we are not looking at you." He held Vanessa's hand and stared unwaveringly at Denzil Ingram. "A small act of self-indulgence that will make you feel warmer. Right?"

"Wrong," said Ingram. "Put on your clothes, Dr. Badel. Vanessa will tell you that I don't intend to shoot while you are zipping up your trousers. She will doubtless confirm that I am also trying rather hard to think of an alternative."

Vanessa looked at Roland and nodded. They began to dress. While they did so, Denzil Ingram went on talking.

"We have no time to speak delicately or — as they used to say when I was young — beat about the bush. My mission, as Vanessa knows, is to take her out. And, since you have become involved with her, Dr. Badel, unhappily that also includes you."

118

"We live in a nice world," commented Roland, putting on his trousers and a shirt, but contriving all the time to face Ingram. "What has she done that is so terrible? Has she hit an old lady with an iron bar? Has she probed somebody in possession of state secrets? Has she tapped Joe Humboldt's erotic dreams?"

Ingram sighed. "Let us take the bit about justice as read, Dr. Badel. Vanessa is not old enough; but you know and I know that justice is a chimera. All Vanessa has done is to jump school. Alas, in doing so, she has become a Parliamentary Question. Upon her existence or non-existence depends the fate of a Bill and quite possibly the fate of a government. I am paid to protect the state and the government. Do you see my problem?"

"Perfectly. But how do you sleep at nights?"

"Quite well, thank you. I have my anodynes . . . Incidentally, I have sent my men away. I tell you this, Dr. Badel, not to raise hope but so that you may understand my position before we talk. It is routine procedure these days. They found what I wanted them to find — but they did not know quite what I was looking for. A sensible precaution. If any of them are probed, they can reveal only that I sought a man with a disfigured face. They cannot reveal, subsequently, if that man lived or died, or even if he had a companion. Do I make myself clear?"

"Damnably clear." Roland's voice was rising, though he tried desperately to remain calm. "What is the scenario? Unknown lovers die in suicide pact — or will you burn the house afterwards and create a temporary local mystery?"

Vanessa had finished dressing. She came to Roland. He held her close, stroked her hair.

"There are several possible scenarios, as you are

119

pleased to call them, Dr. Badel. But let us talk."

Roland could not contain his anger. "Is that your private kick, man? Have you sunk so low that you need to see your victims squirm?"

Ingram sighed. It should have been so easy. But it was not going as planned. If only he had burst into the room and killed without thinking. It was a fatal mistake to think too much. He was getting old.

"Tell him, Vanessa. This time I will open to you. Tell him what you find."

Vanessa closed her eyes momentarily. Then she turned to Roland Badel. "He found us — or you — through my mother. She has been in rapport with me. She had an image of a man with a disfigured face. He had decided to kill my mother and her husband after he had killed me. But now he is not sure what to do. He — he wants to avoid the killing, if he can."

"Why?" Roland could not understand it.

Vanessa shot a questioning glance at Denzil Ingram. "Tell him!"

"He saw me on the bed, defenceless. He saw me as a child. It reminded him of his own childhood . . . He — he, too, was put into a state home because he was unwanted. He had to fight very hard to make his way in the world."

Denzil Ingram said: "Well, Dr. Badel, are you satisfied? I said that I wanted you to understand my position before we talked. I also said that I was not trying to raise any hope. Now, shall we talk or shall I carry out my task as efficiently and painlessly as possible?"

Somehow, Vanessa had suddenly passed beyond fear. Or perhaps she had locked the fear away so deep that she could no longer feel it consciously. "We will talk, Mr. Ingram," she said calmly. "I don't think you want either of us to plead with you. But we will talk."

Ingram kept his hand firmly on the laser pistol in his pocket. "I'm glad, Vanessa. It may get us nowhere, but we will talk. If there is any alternative that does not affect my integrity, I will gladly take it. My mission remains unchanged: to ensure that Vanessa Smith never existed. There is no time for any other route."

"Integrity!" exploded Roland. "You talk of integrity."

Ingram smiled. "Surely, Dr. Badel, as a psychologist you will agree that anyone who remains true to his own values and avowed function preserves subjective integrity?"

Vanessa said: "Tell me about my mother, Mr. Ingram. I would like to have some knowledge of her, even if second-hand."

"She is a very attractive woman, Vanessa. I think you would like her. Fairly tall, slim, very sensitive, volatile. She threw a glass at me and cut my head. Yes, you would like her. She is called Jenny Pargetter. She is in her late thirties. She has short, brown hair, very fine, well looked after. She has a longish face, high cheek bones, large brown eyes, expressive lips. Her husband, Simon, is a prosperous city executive. They obviously love each other very much. In other circumstances, I might count myself lucky if they were my friends."

"Is Simon my father?"

"No. Your father died before you were born. He was, I believe, a young Rhodesian arts graduate. He was killed in a protest brawl near the American Embassy."

"I see. Thank you. Thank you for giving me some memories to treasure. I can invent the rest, Mr. Ingram. You must know that people like us are good at invention."

Roland said: "You spoke of alternatives, Ingram. Have you any to suggest?"

Denzil Ingram shrugged. "I have one. But, from a professional point of view, you may consider the cure to be worse than the disease, so to speak... Have you any whisky?"

"It's downstairs. I'll get it."

Ingram smiled. "Please. I am not in my dotage. We will all go downstairs. You will both go very slowly ahead of me. Let us not have any mistakes. I hate mistakes. They do terrible things to my reflexes."

In the living room, Denzil Ingram settled in an easy chair with a glass of whisky in his hand just as if he were paying a relaxed social call.

"Thank you for the whisky. You will not join me, Dr. Badel?"

"Forgive me. I do not drink with executioners."

"Tut-tut. Such social prejudice — especially in a distinguished psychologist... And you, Vanessa? Are you old enough to drink whisky?"

She gave a faint smile. "I had some earlier. Then I was sick."

"Come to the point, man," said Roland irritably. "Let us hear what, if anything, you have to offer. You may enjoy the suspense. We do not." He glanced at Vanessa, who was very pale. "She has had about as much as she can stand."

Denzil Ingram took a deep breath. "Well, then, let us consider. First, as I have said, it is now necessary that Dr. Roland Badel and Vanessa Smith cease to exist. Second, as Vanessa has discovered, I do not wish to kill you if it can be avoided. Third, imprisonment is out of the question. It carries too many risks. Fourth... Well, Dr. Badel, you at least must realise the alternative."

Roland nodded slowly. "Surgery, brain-washing, synthetic personalities."

"It can be done," said Ingram calmly. "You will know better than I about the recent techniques in brain surgery and personality implantation. I am told it is entirely possible to create new personalities within six weeks."

"Zombies," said Roland. "I have seen case-histories. They live, they function, but what are they?"

Ingram shrugged. "At least they are alive. They can be contented. They can find fulfilment."

"So can laboratory rats — which is what you propose to turn us into. Even you must appreciate that to destroy the personality while preserving the body is simply another kind of death ... And what afterwards? You would have to keep your synthetic Miss X and Mr. Y under surveillance for the rest of their lives in case the shadow personalities emerged."

"That is true. But Miss X and Mr. Y need know nothing of it."

Roland Badel gave a bitter laugh. "Miss X and Mr. Y would know nothing about anything that matters. I cannot speak for Vanessa but I can speak for myself. It is not for me, Ingram."

Vanessa said softly. "You must decide for me, also, Roland. I know it's a great responsibility. But I need to feel that someone is responsible for me in my life, and even in my death. Forgive me for bringing all this on you. I'm sorry."

Roland pressed her hand. Then he turned to Denzil Ingram. "There is another solution. The simple one. Let us go, say, to South America — a country of your choosing. Give us passports and new names. Keep us under surveillance if you must. We will not make trouble."

Ingram shook his head slowly. "I'm sorry. It is tempting. But the risks are too great. The Opposition will do everything they can to find Vanessa. If they succeed, my head is on the block ... Have you any other suggestions, Dr. Badel?"

"There is an induced amnesia technique that — "

"Not on. My department has experimented with it. The effects are unpredictable — as you must know, of course." Ingram seemed genuinely sad as he spoke.

"I have just thought of something," said Vanessa, her voice trembling. "It seems that I alone am the real problem, Mr. Ingram. If you kill me and — " her voice faltered, "destroy the evidence, as I am sure you know how, there can be no need to kill Dr. Badel."

"You would do this for him?" There was a note of respect in Denzil Ingram's voice.

"I love him, you see. Besides," she smiled at Roland, "if I had not tried to steal eggs from his hens, you would not now be here. I realise I have to die. I don't know very much about the political situation that makes my death necessary, and I don't want to know. But, surely, when I am gone there is no real evidence that I ever lived, you would not need to kill Roland or my mother or her husband ... Even if they would not give you their word, I am sure they would give it to me."

Dr. Roland Badel said nothing. He did not trust himself to speak. There were tears on his face. It was a strange sensation. Inconsequentially, he tried to remember when he had last wept.

Denzil Ingram took the laser pistol out of his pocket. He looked at it for a moment or two, then placed it on the small table by his chair.

"I am getting old, Vanessa. I have lived by my own code for more years than I care to remember. Survival of the fittest." He smiled. "It seemed a good code. A classic code, in fact. But when a young girl can make me doubt its worth, I realise I have outlived my values."

He looked at Roland. "Dr. Badel, you suggested South America."

"I did," said Roland evenly.

"Can you arrange passports, money, etcetera?"

"I think so."

"Good. May I recommend Chile or Peru. We do not have particularly good relations with either country at the moment. I think you could establish new identities there without too much difficulty . . . I am now going to pour myself a rather large whisky. I am also going to smoke a cigarette. I am getting careless in my dotage. You see my laser pistol. I would be greatly indebted if you do not use it until I put my empty glass down. You will aim a little to the left of my spine and a foot below the shoulder. Is that agreed?"

"It is agreed, Mr. Ingram," said Roland Badel, amazed. "I still do not drink with executioners; but it would be a great privilege to drink with a brave man. May I pour the whisky?"

"No, Dr. Badel," said Ingram with a tight smile. "Indulge a foible, please. It is my privilege also not to drink with my executioner."

Vanessa said fiercely: "Must it end like this? Must somebody die? Is the world entirely mad?"

"Yes, Vanessa," said Ingram, "the world is entirely mad, and somebody must die." Then he added fiercely: "Leave me my pride, please. It is all I have left . . . Now, no more words, please, from either of you. I wish to enjoy my whisky."

He got up, went to the antique sideboard, lifted the decanter and poured his whisky. He took a sip, rolling the fluid round his mouth, savouring it, trying not to think of anything but memories — the few good times he had known: a toboggan ride down a Derbyshire hillside one Christmas long, long ago, with a man who

125

seemed to know all about him and might or might not have been his father; his first job, making tea for mysterious men in a secret government department, men who talked nonchalantly of exotic places like Sofia, Belgrade, Lisbon, Istanbul, Bangkok; a woman called Elise who had once taught him much about love in the most squalid circumstances in Marseilles. On the whole, he reflected, it had been an interesting life, if a lonely one. There was some amusement to be derived from the knowledge that he was voluntarily surrendering it, at a point when his career could be greatly advanced, in the English South Downs. Damn Vanessa! She was the daughter he would have liked to have had, if there had been time . . .

Denzil Ingram never finished his whisky.

Roland Badel never became his executioner.

Vanessa never found peace in South America.

As Ingram took his second sip of the whisky, a pane of glass shattered in the cottage window and a small blue sphere fell upon the carpet.

Vanessa looked at it, Roland looked at it, Denzil Ingram looked at it. He alone knew what it was. But by then it was already too late. The sphere dissolved, and there was an explosive puff of vapour. And then for the three of them there was nothingness.

17

VANESSA OPENED HER eyes. At first, she couldn't focus. But when she did manage to see clearly she found that there were three strangers in the room. No, not entirely strangers because, weak though she was, she managed to flash probe and found two of the thought patterns horribly familiar.

She saw a mishapen boy, a girl with hungry and malignant eyes, a white-haired old man. Superficially, the white-haired old man looked like everyone's notion of an eccentric grandfather. But there was a coldness about him. A deadly coldness. The coldness of an animal that strikes to kill.

"Welcome, Vanessa," said Quasimodo. "You are welcome to my thoughts. Soon you will have as many as you can handle."

"Hello, girlie," said Janine with malice. "It was not a bad screw, considering your equipment. Why the hell did you have to be sick?"

Professor Raeder said: "You are extraordinarily lucky, Vanessa. You may not believe it at the moment, but we are your friends." He held out Denzil Ingram's laser pistol in his hand. "We arrived, it seems, at the right moment. It would have been rather frustrating to find you dead."

Vanessa said nothing. She set up as strong a mental

block as she could, then she looked at Roland and Denzil Ingram. Both were unconscious, lying on the floor. Each of them had his wrists bound together with what seemed to be fine, strong wire.

Professor Raeder noted her glance. "They are alive, Vanessa. No doubt they will join us presently ... But let me reassure you. Your troubles are now over, my dear. You are about to join my sociable little group of paranormals, and together we shall work constructively to overthrow the reactionary government now ruling this country. Together, we few, by our decisive actions, will reassert the ancient tradition of democracy in this land. History will be kind to us, Vanessa. We shall doubtless be compared with that glorious few who withstood the might of Nazi tyranny several decades before you were born. Theirs was a battle of the air. Ours will be a battle of the spirit. But I can assure you it will be no less wonderful."

"Who are you?" Vanessa managed to say. She suddenly realised that she was sitting in her chair and that her hands were not tied. She felt an impulse to get up and run. But she knew that she would not get very far. She gritted her teeth and prayed that Roland would soon be conscious. Perhaps he would know what to do.

"I am sorry. Forgive me. Marius Raeder. Professor Emeritus of Paranormal Psychology at the University of Cambridge, lately retired. My untimely retirement was brought about by the attentions of Sir Joseph Humboldt's minions — one of whom, if I am not mistaken, slumbers peacefully by your paramour."

Vanessa was little the wiser. This strange man used strange words that she did not understand. But she knew beyond any doubt that he was evil.

Professor Raeder sighed. "I see my name means

nothing to you. But why should it? They would not tell you at Random Hill that the work of Marius Raeder was basically responsible for their entire programme. I was to have received a Nobel Prize, my dear. But that is beside the point, and it is a sad story. Sufficient to say that you are now in good hands. Your talents will be appreciated and rewarded correspondingly. You will come with us to Scotland, and all will be well."

"I don't want to go anywhere at all with you . . . Please . . . please just leave me alone."

Raeder smiled. "I'm sorry, dear child. I can't do that. I know your psychoprofile, you see. Intimately, I may say. You are absolutely essential to my plans. You have a talent, a rare talent, of which you are not yet aware. You are my burning glass."

Roland returned to consciousness abruptly and with a sudden jerk, as if someone had struck him or shouted at him. He tried to get up, discovered that his hands were bound and managed to struggle into a sitting position. He shook his head as if to dismiss residual effects of the anaesthetic gas, and looked round. He was visibly relieved to see that Vanessa was apparently unharmed.

"What the devil is all this about?" he demanded of Raeder.

"Ah, Dr. Badel, you have joined us. I am so pleased to see you. May I introduce myself. I am — "

"Don't bother. I know you, Professor Raeder. I attended enough of your lectures. What is going on?"

"He wants to take me to Scotland," said Vanessa. She shivered. "He talks about things I don't understand."

Denzil Ingram also showed signs of returning consciousness. He groaned, struggled to move his hands, then sat up suddenly. He saw Marius Raeder. "I know you."

"And I know you, Mr. Ingram. I need hardly add that our brief meeting will not be to your advantage. I have already tolerated more than enough inconvenience from Humboldt's dogs."

Surprisingly, Ingram laughed. "I have a taste for irony. If you had tossed your gas bomb five minutes later, Professor Raeder, I would have already been dead."

"Rest easy," retorted the Professor. "Your destiny will not be long frustrated. That I promise."

Denzil Ingram looked calmly around him. "There are several witnesses, Raeder. It is unfortunate — not for me, for you. Sooner or later you will have to destroy them all, or one of them — quite possibly that thing — " he glanced at Quasimodo, "will destroy you."

"Let me have him," said Quasimodo. "I'd like to play with him Professor. I'd like that very much."

Professor Raeder sighed. "Child, try to develop a sense of proportion. We have more important things to do than torment stray dogs."

"What is so important to you, Professor Raeder?" said Ingram. "You have come for Vanessa, that is plain. But why is she so important to you?"

Professor Raeder pointed the pistol at Denzil Ingram. "Your time is rapidly running out," he said calmly. "But there's no reason why a dead man should not briefly be entrusted with the confidence of the living. I intend to assassinate Sir Joseph Humboldt, who has brought this country to the edge of totalitarianism and myself to great discredit. I intend to destroy his government and all he stands for. Vanessa is my burning glass. I do not think you will understand the implications. And so, I bid you good night."

Professor Raeder held the pistol steady, pressed the trigger. It was all over in a second. A tiny, steaming hole appeared in Denzil Ingram's forehead. His eyes widened as if in wonder. Then he uttered a great sigh and fell back dead. And then there was the acrid smell of burnt tissue. Vanessa could not cope with the experience on top of all that had happened. She gave a thin cry, vainly tried to cover her face with her hands, and slumped back in a faint.

"That wasn't much fun," complained Quasimodo.

"It was not my intention to entertain," snapped Professor Raeder. He glanced at Vanessa. "Bring some water. It seems our new recruit is a sensitive plant."

Roland Badel, pale, trembling, tried to control his emotions. "That was a pretty callous act, Professor Raeder. I would have preferred to remember you not as a psychopath but as the brilliant man who once inspired hundreds of students."

"He's lovely when he's angry," observed Janine. "I could eat him. I really could."

Raeder ignored her. "My dear Badel, thank you for the back-handed compliment. But I fear your values are distorted by stress. I have simply put down a dog — one of Humboldt's dogs. If you have any knowledge of what is happening in Britain today, you will realise upon reflection that I have just carried out an act of social justice. Incidentally, I imagine that our late friend's mission was to take out you and Vanessa. Am I correct?"

"You are correct."

"Then I have done you a service, Dr. Badel. You are indebted to me."

"No, Professor Raeder, you have done me a great disservice. Before you came, tossing a gas bomb through the window, Denzil Ingram had reneged upon his

131

mission. At the cost of his own life, he would have allowed us to leave this country and begin a new life elsewhere."

"So? The dog turned upon its master. An amusing thought."

"I was not talking of a dog, Professor Raeder. I was talking of a man."

"Badel," said the Professor, "if you wish to live, do not annoy me. Your continued existence depends upon myself and Vanessa. Keep her happy, persuade her to co-operate, and you may remain alive. Please remember that. I shall, I hope, not need to remind you."

Quasimodo returned from the kitchen with a jug of water.

"Give me that," said Janine. With a malicious smile, Janine poured half the water over Vanessa's face. She sat up, spluttering and coughing.

"Hello again, girlie," said Janine. "My! You've had a hard day's night, haven't you?"

"That gesture was quite unnecessary," said Raeder. "In future, Janine, you will do absolutely nothing without my approval. Vanessa is to be our friend and associate, a willing member of our dedicated group. So far, you have only managed to alienate her. You are nearer the electrodes than you think."

Janine sat down, white-faced, mumbling to herself.

Vanessa looked at Denzil Ingram, shuddered, then met Roland's gaze. She saw anguish in his eyes. No doubt, she thought, there was anguish in hers also.

"Are you all right, Roland?"

"Of course he's all right, child," snapped the Professor. "All I have done is to remove one of your enemies. You should be grateful for that."

Wet, cold, miserable, exhausted, Vanessa somehow managed to confront Professor Raeder with courage.

"I am grateful to you for nothing. I hate what you have done, and now I know you to be utterly evil. If I could have known that I would have been the cause of so much tragedy, I would have stayed at Random Hill and done whatever they asked of me."

Professor Raeder smiled. "Well spoken. I disagree with your juvenile analysis, of course; but I like your spirit." He glanced at Janine and Quasimodo. "One has to work with the material available. Sometimes, it is very trying... However, I trust you will be tolerant, Vanessa. Together, we can accomplish great things."

"If you think I would willingly help someone who can — "

"I think you will help." Raeder lifted the pistol once more and pointed it at Roland's forehead. "I think you will help whether he lives or dies."

Roland and Vanessa looked at each other. His eyes seemed curiously remote, almost as if he had suddenly become a stranger. "I think," he said softly, "it will be better for you if I remain alive."

Vanessa gave a great sigh — of misery and defeat.

"I'm glad we have settled the problem amicably," said Professor Raeder with conscious irony. "Now we must leave here with all haste, before the other dogs return. We have a long way to travel; but I assure you that my hovercar is well equipped. May I suggest, Vanessa, that you change into some dry clothes. A bad cold at this time would interfere somewhat with my plans. You may also pack a few small necessities for yourself and dear Dr. Badel. Janine will help you. We are going to a place where shopping facilities are, I fear, restricted."

"The Scottish Highlands," said Vanessa dully. "That is where you wanted me to go, isn't it?"

"Ah, yes. I'm so glad you got the message. We tried,

133

of course, to set up a compulsion pattern. But there was not a great deal of time available."

Quasimodo looked at Roland. "Professor, let's take him out. He is trouble. I just flashed him. He is real trouble. Besides, I'd like to see him die. Let me do it."

"Bloodthirsty child," observed the Professor. "Perhaps I will eventually indulge you, but not just now. You miss the point, Quasimodo. While Vanessa lives and is not in danger, Dr. Badel will be most obliging. While Dr. Badel lives and is not in danger, Vanessa will be most obliging. We could not have a more satisfactory arrangement . . . Do you agree with my analysis, Dr. Badel?"

"Yes, Professor Raeder. I would have phrased it differently, perhaps, but that is the case."

"I am glad we are in accord. Incidentally, Dr. Badel, I hope you are comprehensively insured. I have it in mind to burn your house when we leave. It will not confuse the dogs greatly, I fear, but it will certainly delay them. There will have to be forensic analysis and all that sort of thing — particularly when the charred body is discovered. The law is an ass; but sometimes an ass can be useful. We will monitor the newscasts, and I will keep you informed."

"Professor Raeder," said Roland, "I could not wish to be in the hands of a more considerate man."

Raeder smiled. "I am so glad you see it my way, Dr. Badel."

134

18

JENNY AND SIMON PARGETTER were back in their own home, trying to adjust to what had happened to them, trying to adjust to the threats that had been made, the bargain that had been struck.

They felt like lost souls, like prisoners on parole. And, somehow, perhaps because of the forced probes, the ensuing humiliation, the bitter knowledge that they had had to buy their own lives and Vanessa's life — or so they tried to believe — with a promise of silence, they felt strangely unclean.

Simon, still youthful and attractive, though past the critical age of forty, had led a more sheltered life than Jenny. He came from a prosperous family and had almost automatically found a highly-paid job that enabled him to live in some luxury. Freedom was something he had always taken for granted. Whatever happened to poor people, or presumptuous people or over-ambitious people, he and his kind had always led a satisfying and unrestricted life. They, the upper middle class, the managerial stratum, had been accustomed to accept security and freedom as a kind of built-in birthright.

For the first time in his life, he had come up against the power of depersonalised Authority. He had been confronted with, and processed by, a power that he could not resist, buy, or compromise with. The effect was traumatic. He had learned, for the first time, that he was neither secure nor free.

He enjoyed drinking, social drinking. He liked a good wine with his dinner, a brandy with his coffee. But he was not a drunkard, or had not been until now. As he poured himself a fourth large whisky, drinking it neat, Jenny registered the level in the bottle and took note of the clinical symptoms.

"I think I had better join you, Simon. If you are going to get pissed out of your mind, I ought to be in a similar condition. Then neither of us will notice how stupid or repulsive the other one is."

"Darling, forgive me. I ought to be cheering you up. But, you see, I have to cheer myself up first— or get stoned enough not to care too much." He poured her drink. "Ice? Water? American Dry?"

"As it is, darling. I want to catch up."

Simon handed her the tumbler. "The thing is, with someone like Ingram, how can we be sure he means what he says? To be successful in the kind of work he does, you have to be prepared to obtain results at any price."

Jenny took a large swallow of whisky and then gave a bitter laugh. "I always suspected that beneath your gay exterior there lay a thinking man. No, erase that, darling. I don't want to be bitchy... Of course, we can't be sure of anything Ingram promised. But the only way to get out of that infernal place seemed to be to pretend to accept his bargain on its face value."

"So there still remains the possibility that they might take Vanessa out, and us also, as a possible source of embarrassment."

"It's an evens chance, I think." Jenny finished her drink. "More, please."

136

Simon filled both glasses. "Then we must do some contingency planning."

"Contingency planning! That is a nice executive phrase. How can we plan for the contingency of our dying, Mr. Executive? Take out more insurance?"

"Be constructive, sweetheart. If we are both going to fall flat after a booze session or wake up on the morning after to find some anonymous character ready to fill us full of laser holes, we need to be constructive."

Jenny smiled. "It's a good word. I like it. It's a reassuring word. But how are we to be constructive, Simon? The clock ticks loud."

Simon scratched his head. "An immediate precaution would be to write down all we know and deposit the statement at the bank, to be made public in the event of our deaths."

"I think, somehow, Joe Humboldt's boys would find a way of corrupting the incorruptible bank."

"Then the same statement goes to our lawyers also."

"Likewise." Jenny drank deeply.

"We also tape the statement and send a copy to each of our friends, with instructions what to do."

"You dislike our friends so much that you will put them at risk?"

"Dammit, we have to do something!" he expostulated.

"Yes, we have to do something." Jenny held out her empty glass. "Give me another, then take me to bed and screw me stupid, while you can still perform. Make it so that I can't think, feel, or remain conscious. Give me oblivion ... Dear Simon, I do love you, and I am sorry I brought all this on your head."

He kissed her. "I love you, too, Jenny. After all these years, you are still an exciting woman. There is no need to apologise for Vanessa."

"I'm not apologising for Vanessa ... I'm apologising

137

for me. According to some long-dead poet — Andrew Marvell, I imagine — the grave's a fine and private place, but none, I think, do there embrace. Let's go to bed."

"I want to. But what about Denzil Ingram?"

"Forget Denzil Ingram. Let's go to bed and try to make love. Or, if we can't make love, at least we can hold each other very close."

"Darling, we can't just dismiss him."

"We can't. Someone else has."

"How do you know?"

Jenny drank more whisky. "How do you think I know ... Poor Vanessa! Somehow, I seem to be getting more and more finely tuned to her. It's something I want, and it is something terrible. Come to bed, and I'll tell you about it."

Suddenly, hope seemed to flash across Simon's face. "Then if Ingram is dead, we might be — "

Slowly, Jenny shook her head. "Think. It doesn't work like that. *Le roi est mort: vive le roi.* Hold me close, Simon. Hit me, revile me, make love to me. But hold me close. I need to prove that I am myself, Jenny Pargetter. I need to know that I am alive."

Sir Joseph Humboldt was, as usual, taking breakfast in his dressingroom at Ten, Downing Street. And, as usual, while he ate he discussed matters of the day with Dick Haynes, his Private Secretary.

"So Tom Green has another awkward P.Q. for me, has he?" Sir Joseph was eating his accustomed breakfast of sausages and bacon and egg. He drowned the sausages in tomato ketchup until they looked like the bodies of small rodents foully done to death, then he speared one on his fork and munched away with evident relish.

Haynes suppressed a shudder. His own breakfast had consisted of grapefruit, toast and coffee.

"Yes, sir. Question forty-two: To ask the Prime Minister, who has already assured the House that Vanessa Smith, alleged to have been detained at Random Hill Residential School, does not exist, if he is aware that Dugal Nemo, also an inmate of Random Hill, has committed suicide as a result of duress."

Sir Joseph popped the rest of the sausage into his mouth and briefly evinced satisfaction.

"Two for the price of one, Dick. I like Tom Green. He's a great fighter, But clearly he will have to be stopped . . . Ingram is dead, I understand."

"Yes, sir."

"And Vanessa Smith got away?"

"Yes, sir."

"And now we have the additional embarrassment of this child Dugal Nemo. It is a very nasty situation. I do not care for it overmuch . . . Could we prove that Dugal Nemo did not exist?"

"We could, sir. But it would be inadvisable."

Sir Joseph gave a cold smile. "I take your point. We must not lose credibility . . . Well, then, could it be shown to be an accident?"

"Sir, the boy hanged himself in a lavatory . . . At least, that is my information."

"I see."

Having disposed of the sausages, Sir Joseph methodically attacked the bacon.

"There is the possibility of murder, I suppose. It would be more acceptable than suicide . . . If Dugal Nemo had been murdered, we could be seen to be rather strong on justice — provided, of course, that we could find a murderer."

"That would be very difficult, Prime Minister," said

Haynes neutrally. "Particularly as it can be shown that no murder was committed."

Sir Joseph looked at his First Secretary. "Dick, you are not a fool — otherwise you would not be holding your present position. You have served me well, and advancement lies just around the corner for you. But it depends upon the success of my policies and my government. In politics, you know that we must sometimes accomplish things that are personally repugnant to us. We are servants of the nation, Dick. It is a heavy responsibility. As private persons, we can care deeply for the liberty of the individual. As people charged with high office, it is our duty above all to consider the security of the country. Do I make myself clear?"

"Lucidly so, sir." Haynes hated himself, hated his weakness. Hated the fact that the Prime Minister knew he was ambitious and played upon the knowledge. But what could one do?

"Well, then," went on Sir Joseph, "let us suppose it was politically necessary to establish a case of murder. Who is the person most likely to be the murderer?"

"Dr. Lindemann," said Haynes, hating himself even more. "He was the one who kicked the lavatory door down and discovered Dugal Nemo's body."

"He is the one who alleges he kicked the door down," amended Sir Joseph, dipping a piece of bacon into the yolk of his egg. "Who is this Dr. Lindemann? What does he do?"

"He has a high reputation, sir. He is in charge of the group of paranormal children which included both Vanessa Smith and Dugal Nemo."

"The fact that two of his child superstars have become a great source of political embarrassment does little to enhance his reputation. Could he be a subversive?"

Haynes fidgeted. "In view of his record, Prime Minister," he said uncomfortably, "it would be a difficult thing to prove."

"But not impossible?"

"No, sir. Not impossible. There are people in S Department who could arrange — "

"Spare me the details. I do not want to know ... If he were a subversive and, perhaps, a sexual pervert, by putting him on trial we could be seen to be championing the rights of gifted children. That would be advantageous. We need to recruit paranormal talent, but we are prepared to throw the book at anyone who endangers it."

"Sir, there is a difficulty. If Dr. Lindemann is placed on trial, he will defend himself by revealing the truth about Vanessa Smith. He will call witnesses from Random Hill, and — "

"Not if he is offered a deal," said Sir Joseph imperturbably. "We need his confession, and we need his guilt. But he needs his life. At least, I imagine he does. That is something we will have to establish before we proceed. But, on the assumption that he wishes to continue living, it should be easy to strike a bargain. If he will confess to being an agent, say, of the Chinese or the Russians; or even, at a pinch, of some emerging African power, we will give him the maximum sentence for the benefit of the record and undertake to exchange him for some non-existent British agent as soon as the affair ceases to be headline news. If Dr. Lindemann values his skin, he will accept the deal."

"And would we honour our side of the bargain, sir?" asked Haynes recklessly.

"Of course," said Sir Joseph, finishing off his egg. "One should always stand by one's word — unless circumstances decree otherwise. However, there are still

141

two troublesome points. I cannot understand why an experienced man like Ingram should have bungled his assignment. He had authority to use whatever force was necessary. His failure disturbs me. The other problem is: who leaked the death of Dugal Nemo?"

"Both mysteries are being investigated, Prime Minister."

"I see. Any results yet?"

"No, sir."

"Who is in charge at Random Hill?'"

"A Professor Holroyd, sir. A distinguished academic."

"There is a file on him?"

"Of course, sir. He is a very distinguished man. He is one of the four who took up where Rhine left off and broke through the psych barrier. When he was younger, he made several significant contributions to the science of personality reshaping. His present post is almost a sinecure. Nominally, he is responsible for the paranormal development programme there. In practice, he is a rubber stamp for people like Lindemann... He is very old, sir."

"Hm... Do we know anything about his politics?"

Haynes smiled. "He is harmless, sir. Almost in his dotage. An old-fashioned liberal."

"Is he, indeed!" Sir Joseph stroked his chin. "Old-fashioned liberals, allegedly in their dotage, have an alarming capacity to bite... Now I know how the news of Dugal Nemo's death was given to Tom Green. Have Professor Holroyd taken out."

"Sir, we cannot destroy a man on supposition."

Sir Joseph Humboldt wiped his lips with his napkin. "We can if I say so, Dick. The safety of the realm is my consideration. Let us reduce the imponderables. Professor Holroyd must be taken out. Then we will see how long Tom Green's ammunition lasts."

19

VANESSA WOKE UP feeling stiff and cold and very hungry. For a few moments she had no idea of where she was or of what had happened. Then the events of the night came back to her. She remembered having her hands bound and then being bundled out of the house, along with Roland, into the still, moonlit night. She remembered being allowed to stand on the dewy grass for a few seconds before being pushed into Professor Raeder's large, safari hovercar.

The moon had been beautiful, the stars had been beautiful; and the cottage where she had found a brief sanctuary looked like an enchanted cottage. If only she could have stayed there for ever! If only she could have had the paranormal powers that had brought such misery burned out of her brain!

Professor Raeder, laser pistol in hand, motioned Roland and Vanessa into the rear of the hovercar while Janine and Quasimodo, taking obvious pleasure in their task, arranged the combustibles that would destroy the only home that Vanessa had ever known.

The fire took a quick, eager hold upon the house. While she was watching the flames leap hungrily in the bedroom and the lounge, with the front door left open to increase the draught, Roland tried to say something to her; but he didn't manage it. He gave a great sigh, and his head sank into his chest. Vanessa felt a slight pricking sensation in her arm. Then she heard Professor Raeder say as if from a great distance: "Sleep well, Vanessa. I envy you. For me there is much work and much thinking to be done. Your exertions will not be required till later."

And then there was nothingness. Until she woke miserable and hungry in a narrow bed in a small room with a barred window. She was fully clothed, but a coverlet had been laid over her. She got up, wincing with the aches in her body, and went over to the window.

All she could see through it were fleecy sunlit clouds in the sky, below, a patch of rough ground that might once have been a garden and a high, dark wall of densely growing pine trees. She stared through the window for a while, seeking life, movement; but there was only sky, forest, grass and a few wild flowers. She stood still and listened, but could not even hear any house noises.

Then she went to the door, and tried to turn the handle. The door would not open. She thought of banging on it or shouting; but she changed her mind, went back to the bed and sat down. She needed to think what would be the best thing to do.

Whatever else he might be, however mad he was, Professor Raeder seemed to be the kind of man who paid great attention to detail. No doubt Roland was locked in a similar kind of room, also wondering what to do.

She closed her eyes, formed a mental image of Marius Raeder, groping for rapport, and tried a flash probe.

She heard a loud chuckle which seemed to come from the centre of the room. She opened her eyes with a start, almost expecting to see Raeder. But there was no one.

"Good afternoon, Vanessa. I should have warned you

that one of the rules of the house is that I am not to be probed. Transgression carries the risk of a somewhat painful punishment. However, you are new here, and must be forgiven an indiscretion or two. I trust you are well rested?"

"Where are you?"

"Elsewhere, obviously. That is all you need to know. I can see you, but you can't see me." Again the dreadful chuckle. "I hope you like your room, Vanessa. I chose it for the pleasing view. Kindly bear in mind that you can be observed at all times. It may help to inhibit any foolishness."

"Where is Roland?" She knew it was a mistake to ask, to betray her concern, but she could not help it.

"How touching," observed the Professor. "Your first thoughts are for his safety. It almost restores my faith in human nature. Don't worry, child. I am no ogre. Dr. Badel is still asleep in his room. No harm has come to him, and none will if you co-operate fully."

"How long do you intend to keep us here?"

"Not very long, my dear. At least, I hope not very long. It depends on how good you are, how much telergy you can contain and focus. I may say that I have high hopes, very high hopes. Yours is a unique psychoprofile. You are quite extraordinarily receptive. I doubt if there is another paranormal of your capacity in the whole of Europe ... Well, if your powers are as good as I think they are, you and Dr. Badel will be free to go your own ways quite soon."

"What is telergy?"

"Good gracious! I see they did not attend greatly to your education at Random Hill. But do not worry, Vanessa. We shall shortly have a tutorial, and all will be made clear."

"I'm very hungry. Also I am rather cold."

"There is a temperature control by the side of your bed. It is very efficient. You can turn your room into a refrigerator or a sauna. Janine will bring you some food shortly."

"When can I see Roland?"

"At the tutorial, my dear. As soon as you have eaten and refreshed yourself, we will all gather together and you will meet the other members of our little group. Please do not worry. I am sure you will find us all quite friendly and reasonably informal."

"You are mad, Professor Raeder!" As soon as she had spoken, Vanessa regretted it. This was not the way to help either herself or Roland.

Professor Raeder was amused. "My dear, dear Vanessa, how does one objectively define madness? To paraphrase Bertrand Russell, a philosopher of some merit, I am imaginative, you are eccentric, he is stark staring mad... Have no fears, little one. My madness — if it is such — is a contained madness. I require from you only some small services. If you render them to the best of your ability, I am mad enough to let you and Dr. Badel go free... Till the tutorial, then."

20

IT WAS DARK before Vanessa was let out of her room. Janine came for her, displaying contempt and dislike, as she had done at their first physical encounter. For some reason that Vanessa could not understand, Janine seemed to despise her. She tried a flash probe. Janine slapped her face hard, taking pleasure in the red mark that showed rapidly on her cheek.

"So now you know, girlie."

"Yes, now I know."

It wasn't contempt. It was only hatred. Janine thought that Vanessa was beautiful and that she herself was ugly.

"I may not be a walking talking doll, girlie. But I've got better tits than you have. I respond better. I know what it's all about."

Vanessa held back the tears, determined not to cry. "I'm sure you know what it's all about, Janine. I really know very little. There hasn't been much time... Must we be enemies?"

Janine laughed. "Yes, girlie. We are natural enemies. Nothing can change that. I'm going to take your Roland away from you — one way or another. Now you had better come downstairs with me. Prof doesn't like to be kept waiting."

She was taken down into a large room where two

electric table lamps provided just enough light for everything and everyone to be seen clearly. The furniture was old-fashioned, well worn, and comfortable. One wall was almost entirely covered by well-filled book shelves. In a corner of the room there were various pieces of electronic equipment, some of which Vanessa recognised as being similar to equipment that Dr. Lindemann had used for recording the strength of telepathic transmissions and the level of reception.

There was a large settee, three easy chairs, several upright chairs and two small tables.

Roland sat in one of the easy chairs. He seemed quite relaxed. His hands were untied. Professor Raeder occupied a high-backed upright chair, facing him.

Quasimodo sat in an easy chair near Roland; and a lanky adolescent boy sprawled in a chair on the other side of him. Two strange children, a boy and a girl, had spread themselves out on the settee.

"Ah, Vanessa," said the Professor in a silky tone, "how good of you to join us." There was a laser pistol on the table by his chair. "I have just been explaining our security arrangements to Dr. Badel. He was most attentive. For your benefit, I will repeat them briefly. The house is totally surrounded by proximity mines which I can activate or de-activate electronically. Needless to say, now that we are all gathered together for what might be described as holy communion — " he permitted himself a brief laugh — "the mines will remain continuously active until we have satisfactorily completed our project. I hardly need remind you that you and Dr. Badel will be under continuous surveillance. But if, by chance, one or other of you should venture in an unauthorised fashion from this house, you will be blown to pieces. This I would regret somewhat, but one has to take elementary precautions. However, having

148

disposed of these distasteful preliminaries, let me assure you that your stay with us should be mutually rewarding."

"When can we go, Professor Raeder?" As she spoke, Vanessa cast a glance at Roland His eyes seemed strangely remote.

"When our task is accomplished, Vanessa. It should not take long. Permit me to introduce your colleagues — those you have not already met . . . The young man sitting near Dr. Badel is Alfred. I think you will get on well with him. He has quite a nice nature and is rather good at making and breaking telepathic blocks. Our two young friends on the settee are Robert and Sandra. Robert has some talent for telepathic suggestion and Sandra, on her good days, is capable of telehypnosis. We have to be somewhat patient with Sandra, because she has not yet learned to exercise her powers properly . . . Janine and Quasimodo you have already learned to know and love. So now our little circle is complete."

Roland spoke. "Professor Raeder, Vanessa and I know your aims, and it is my professional opinion that you are mad. But do these — these children understand the kind of risks in which you propose to involve them?"

"These — these childen," repeated Professor Raeder with some irony, "are older than they seem. They fully understand the implications of my project, and they approve. Society has given them a rough deal, Dr. Badel. Society rejected them, then decreed that they should be tools of the state. I have given them back their individuality. They are willing to help me change the present state of affairs and produce a more flexible regime in which they may flourish."

Quasimodo grinned balefully at Roland. "Grow up, stupid. Talk about risks! You're supposed to be a clever bastard, and you don't know nothing. We all get smashed, sooner or later. That's what it's all about. Getting smashed. I been on the receiving end and now I'm going to be on the delivering end. Prof looks after us, ugly face. He knows what we want, and he'll see we get it. So stuff yourself."

Professor Raeder beamed. "The philosophy is a trifle crude, but Quasimodo has a certain primitive eloquence, Dr. Badel. I do not think you will recruit him easily to the ranks of pacifism." He glanced at his watch. "And now there is a little treat in store for us all. In view of the recent political unrest triggered, I imagine, by Vanessa's escape from Random Hill and the subsequent death of a small boy named Dugal Nemo, Sir Joseph Humboldt is speaking to the nation on his Security of the State Bill. In approximately forty-eight hours he will be dead. Let us therefore do him the courtesy of paying some attention to what may well be his final public utterance. Alfred, kindly wheel in the master tri-di and position it so that we can all see clearly. In about forty seconds, the Prime Minister will doubtless move us all with the nobility of his motives."

Obediently, Alfred left the room and returned with a very large tri-di which was mounted on a trolly and obviously did not need an external power source. He positioned it carefully so that everyone could see.

"Turkish delight?" suggested Quasimodo hopefully.

Professor Raeder frowned. "Later, dear child. Turkish delight, at this moment, seems quite inappropriate ... Channel One, Alfred. Please give us maximum definition. I think it is important that we shall see Sir Joseph with great clarity."

Alfred adjusted the controls. The announcer, who was already introducing the Prime Minister, seemed to

150

materialise in the holopix like a perfectly real manikin, three foot tall. It was as if he were actually in the room. Then the cameras switched to Sir Joseph Humboldt. He was seated at his desk at Ten, Downing Street. He looked very calm, very confident, very forceful.

"Good evening," he said. "To everyone, of whatever race, creed or political belief, in this still lovely island of ours, good evening. I speak to you as your Prime Minister and your first servant, of course, but I would greatly prefer to be speaking to you as a friend. Therefore let us forget about internal politics. Indulge my mood. Allow me to talk to you as your friend. I am not seeking votes, nor am I seeking any reward for myself. I am trying to do my duty to you as a friend would, by speaking the truth."

"Splendid!" exclaimed Professor Raeder. "He really does come across beautifully, doesn't he?"

Sir Joseph took a rose from the vase on his desk. He held it in his hand. It was a full, red rose, beautiful. He held it to his nose and sniffed ecstatically. "An English rose, my friends. Wonderful, is it not? But such a rose must be protected if it is to flourish."

He held it a little away from him, and suddenly the petals began to wither. "A trick, my friends, a simple trick. I held the rose in the path of a beam of infra-red radiation. You could not see the beam. You had no means of knowing it was there. The radiation is invisible." He took another rose and held it up, at the same time using his other hand to hold up a transparent shield. The rose remained fresh and full.

"You see, the shield protects this rose . . . I hate to see the destruction of roses. As many of you know, I grow roses in the garden at Number Ten. They soothe me in times of stress . . . Most of all, my friends, I abhor the destruction of the English rose, and I will do all in my power to prevent it."

"Bravo!'" exclaimed Professor Raeder. "An appeal to the heart! Like me he is half-German, of course."

"The rose and the shield are good symbols for the matter which I wish to discuss with you tonight. As you know, in recent years many astounding techniques have been developed in the field of psychology." Sir Joseph laughed. "Like most of you, I do not pretend to understand them. I leave that to the experts. Telepathy has been with us perhaps since the birth of man; but it is only recently that science has enabled us to develop the techniques to exploit it fully. I use the word exploit with some misgivings. It is an ugly but accurate word. Throughout the history of mankind, the more aggressive nations of the world have ruthlessly exploited scientific discoveries for their own ends."

"Your own end, Sir Joseph, is somewhat nearer than you may imagine," interpolated Professor Raeder, rubbing his hands.

"Once it was gunpowder," continued the Prime Minister, "then it became atomic energy and intercontinental missiles and space exploration. Now it is telergy —telepathic energy. I do not need to name to you — indeed, for the sake of diplomacy, I will not — those nations which seek the overthrow of Great Britain's traditional, civilising role in international affairs. Sufficient to say that they are exploiting the new discoveries, telergy and the development of paranormal powers, as a means of strengthening their own positions and destroying the security of others.

"That is why I ask not only Parliament but the entire nation to endorse my Security of the State Bill. By this means we shall be able to recruit all gifted persons with paranormal talent wherever they may be found. They will be the shield that protects the rose. In the new types of psychological warfare which our enemies both at home and abroad are developing, the paranormals will be our Brigade of Guards, an élite corps, commanding our respect, our devotion, our gratitude. We shall look after them well. Make no mistake about that. We shall look after them well, so that they may protect us and help us retain our commanding political position in Europe, our rightful place in world affairs. But it is not only in the field of security and counter-espionage that they will prove — and, indeed, are already proving — their incalculable value. There are, happily, more peaceful, more constructive ways of using their wonderful talents, such as in space communications, in psychotherapy, in teaching, in criminal reform, even in marriage guidance.

"I know that many of you are anxious about your children. You know that teams of government scientists are already visiting schools throughout the country to test for paranormal talent. You are afraid, perhaps, that if your child is found to be gifted, he or she will be whisked away for intensive training.

"Let me assure you of two things. The first is that, to develop paranormal talent to its full, it must be recognised early and trained by experienced people. The second is that, under no circumstances will a child be alienated from its parents. We in this country still have a great reverence for family life and ties. And I can promise you, with my hand on my heart, that the powers we deem necessary to assume for the security of the state will not be abused. Further — "

"Cut!" said Professor Raeder. "Cut this drivel, Alfred, before I get indigestion."

Alfred dutifully manipulated the controls. The tri-di image dissolved. There was a brief silence.

"Well, Vanessa," said Professor Raeder, cheerily, "that is the man we shall shortly destroy. He is the one who, for his own political aims, has publicly announced that you do not exist. He is the one who caused the record of your birth to be erased, ordered your mother to be subjected to humiliating interrogation and made it necessary for you to be murdered. I imagine you will derive some satisfaction when he is taken out."

"I agree with Roland," said Vanessa quietly. "I think you are mad."

"So you are entitled to your opinion, child. But, plainly, you need some encouragement for your role." The Professor smiled at Quasimodo and at Robert and Sandra. "Are you ready to come together, children? We have practised the drill many times."

Quasimodo nodded, with a bored expression.

"Yes, Prof," said Robert. "We are ready."

"Janine, you will reinforce Sandra. Help her if she wavers. Alfred, be ready to break any block that may develop."

Professor Raeder turned to Roland. "Dr. Badel, you are now about to participate in an interesting experiment. We have tried it and succeeded several times with mammals small and large. We have not yet tried it on man. But, personally, I am confident of the result . . .

"Alfred, Janine, Robert, Sandra, Quasimodo, close your eyes now. Seek rapport, find harmony. You are together . . . You have only one will . . . It is my will . . . I will count to five. Then I will utter my command. Execute it instantly. One, two, three, four, five . . . Kill Dr. Badel!" The final words were uttered with great ferocity.

Vanessa gazed at five paranormals, their eyes closed, their faces suddenly drained of expression. "Stop," she called faintly. "Stop this dreadful thing."

154

"There is no stopping it now," said Professor Raeder. "Five is the release word. Watch and take heed."

Roland Badel, utterly surprised by the course of events, tried to rise from his chair. He uttered a strangled cry, shook himself as if he were grappling with some invisible opponent, then sank back. His limbs twitched and shook. His eyes were staring. Strange gobbling noises came from his throat. Then he gave a great sigh and became limp. His eyes remained wide open, sightless.

"It appears that Dr. Badel is now clinically dead, Vanessa," said Professor Raeder calmly. "Personally, I had no doubts about the outcome. But confirmation is always gratifying." He glanced at his wristwatch. "You have about three minutes in which to manifest total enthusiasm for the elimination of Sir Joseph Humboldt."

21

"PLEASE! PLEASE!" CRIED Vanessa. "What do you want me to do?" She gazed round her in horror and misery, unable to glance again at Roland's body, at the sightless eyes, at the fixed and terrible expression on his face.

The young paranormals had opened their eyes once more. Alfred looked puzzled. Janine now wore a petulant expression. Quasimodo treated Vanessa to a malicious smile. Robert and Sandra gazed with unrestrained curiosity at the body.

"Well, we did it, Prof," said Quasimodo. "Nothing to it, really. Like you keep telling us, all we need is harmony and will."

"I did not doubt your ability, children," said Professor Raeder benignly. "But the result is quite spectacular. To have one's theories confirmed with such — such precision is most gratifying."

Hardly knowing what she was doing, Vanessa went on her knees before Professor Raeder.

"Please, please help him! Please do something. I know you can. Please!"

"Do you still think me mad, Vanessa?"

"Yes. No! I don't know. I don't know anything at all. Please help him."

"You think a madman, a person not in possession of his faculties, could develop such a perfect technique?"

156

She rocked to and fro, the tears streaming from her eyes. "I don't know! I don't know. Please don't torment me. I know you have great power ... Give him back his life. I'll do anything. Only give him back his life!"

"What a soft cow," said Janine. Professor Raeder silenced her with a glance.

Then he turned to Vanessa. "Death is an interesting phenomenon," he observed. "Consider Dr. Badel. His heart has stopped. Shortly, his brain cells, deprived of oxygen will begin the irreversible process of corruption. On the other hand, his beard will continue to grow for several hours, and it will take some time before the micro-organisms in his alimentary canal are affected by the demise of their host. Yes, death is an interesting phenomenon."

"Please," moaned Vanessa, "I can't bear any more. Help him. I'll do anything you ask, anything at all."

"A *carte blanche* offer," observed the Professor. "How gratifying. I hardly required as much ... You will do exactly as I say, Vanessa, irrespective of whether you consider me sane or mad?"

"Yes, yes!"

"You will obey me at all times, precisely, and in every detail, knowing that I can use the powers you have seen demonstrated as I choose?"

"Yes. Please, Professor Raeder. I beg you. Help him."

Professor Raeder yawned, glanced at his watch. "Then remember your promise, Vanessa. Remember also the consequences of breaking it ... Alfred, you will find a small black case on the top of my desk. Please bring it to me. I fear I am indulgent enough to be the resurrection and the life. The late Dr. Badel has between fifty and ninety seconds of pseudo-death left. After that, it is likely to be somewhat permanent." He turned to Dr. Badel's body and, unmoved by the sightless gaze, began carefully unbuttoning the dead man's shirt. Vanessa remained on her knees, frozen, watching with an expression in which horror mingled with hope.

Alfred dutifully brought the black case. Professor Raeder unfastened it sufficiently to extract two heavily insulated lengths of flex, each of which was connected to a box inside the case and had a flat copper disc, the size of a penny, at its terminal. Professor Raeder inspected a small dial, visible through a hole cut into the case, then set an external lever carefully and pressed a stud. There was a very faint whirring sound.

"The cardiac stimulator takes about eight seconds to charge," he said conversationally to Vanessa. "Ideally, Dr. Badel's skin should be moist for maximum conductivity. I shall pass the charge into his body here and here." He indicated spots just below the dead man's nipples and slightly more central on his body. He gazed at Vanessa with a faintly malicious smile. "Perhaps you would like to touch the areas with your tongue. Or, if you do not feel up to it, I am sure Janine will oblige."

Dumbly, Vanessa did as she was asked. She was oddly amazed at how warm the flesh still was. She wondered at her own surprise.

"Thank you," said Professor Raeder. "A splendid mechanism, the heart. So simple. A most brilliantly designed pump. Give it a kick and it stops. Give it another kick and it re-starts. At least, let us hope so."

He pressed the copper terminals on the flesh that Vanessa had moistened. Roland's limbs jerked convulsively, his chest heaved, his eyelids fluttered. Professor Raeder lifted the terminals, but the body slumped once more, still lifeless.

"Oh, dear," said Professor Raeder mildly. "Dr.

Badel seems reluctant to return to us. I shall have to increase the voltage."

"Hurry, please hurry," said Vanessa. The phrase 'irreversible process of corruption' seemed to be written into her mind in letters of fire.

Again Professor Raeder consulted the dial, adjusted the regulator lever and pressed the charge button.

He looked at Vanessa. "Another eight seconds, my dear ... You will keep your promise?"

"I will keep my promise. If he lives."

"And if he does not live?"

She stood up, eyes blazing. "I will kill you, or I will die trying. I hate you!"

"So. We truly understand each other. I thought we might. I need you and you need me. Remember that always ... Now, have no fear Vanessa. Dr. Badel is about to rejoin us."

"You were not trying!" Vanessa looked at him, her eyes wide.

"On the contrary, I was succeeding. But now let us see to our late companion."

Once more, Professor Raeder applied the terminals. Again Roland's limbs jerked, his eyes fluttered and his chest heaved. But this time he continued to breathe when the terminals were removed. His heart continued to beat and he was returned almost instantaneously to full consciousness.

He lay pale and weak in the chair, staring dully about him.

Professor Raeder smiled. "Welcome, as they say, to the land of the living. Please don't move or exert yourself for a while, Dr. Badel. Your heart — as you must know — needs a little time to adjust. And in order to set your mind — or should I say brain? — at rest, you will be happy to know that you were resuscitated well

159

within the acceptable limits. There will be no permanent damage."

"Doc, what did it feel like to be dead?" enquired Quasimodo with malicious interest. "I think I like this game. We could keep on killing you, and the Prof could keep on bringing you back. I wonder how long you would last?"

Roland ignored him. "Professor Raeder, you are a clever and ruthless man, and you have reduced us to the level of puppets. But even you must realise that you cannot evade retribution. Come back to reality. You have demonstrated unprecedented control of telergetic power. Publish an account of your researches and techniques and you will be regarded as the greatest parapsychologist of this century. Leave it at that."

Vanessa stroked his forehead, held his hand. "Roland, please don't antagonise him. Please don't. I can't bear any more of this."

Roland sighed. "What did he demand as the price of my life?"

"Absolute obedience. I promised. I will keep the promise as long as you live."

"You paid too much. I'm not worth it. Also, you should be old enough to know that the devil always cheats on his bargains."

Professor Raeder laughed. "Pacts with the devil? My dear Dr. Badel, the trauma of death has clearly distorted your perception somewhat. I trust you will regain your sense of proportion after you have rested. Also, if my knowledge of literature and mythology serves me aright, the devil is renowned for keeping his bargains — to the letter . . . Now, it is my professional opinion — as you know, I also have a degree in medicine — that you should enjoy relaxed rest for several hours. Alfred, dear boy, will assist you to your room, and I will come along later and give you a mild sedative. The heart is a curious machine, tough yet vulnerable — as is the brain. Interrupt its function, however briefly, and you introduce the possibility of psychosomatic feedback. But I am sure you know all this. So, to bed with you, Dr. Badel. Tomorrow, perhaps, if you feel up to it, as the first man to experience telergetic euthanasia, you may care to give me a subjective account of the experience for the record ... Come now, let us help you to your feet. Please enable me to keep my devil's bargain with Vanessa by not trying to do anything quickly for a time."

"May I go with him?" asked Vanessa.

"You may, child. But when you have seen that he is comfortable, you will return here. I must explain to you exactly what is needed to accomplish the destruction of Sir Joseph Humboldt."

When Roland tried to stand up, he realised how weak he was. The psychological trauma that he had experienced was making itself apparent. Sweat broke out on his forehead. He wobbled uncertainly on his legs, like a drunken man, steadied by Alfred and Vanessa.

"You see?" said Professor Raeder. "It has all been just a shade too much for you. But, with a good night's sleep behind you, you will feel like a new man." He laughed. "Yes, positively like a new man. À bientôt, Dr. Badel."

Roland tried to say something. But his chest heaved and his heart pounded, and the words would not form. He allowed himself to be helped out of the room by Vanessa and Alfred. He had been dead; and now he was alive once more. But the life to which he had returned seemed like a kind of dying.

22

WHEN VANESSA RETURNED to Professor Raeder, she found that the others had been dismissed. Alfred, who came back with her, was dismissed also.

"I trust Dr. Badel is now resting?"

"He is in bed, Professor Raeder. I don't know if he is resting."

"Well, I will attend to him presently. You need have no fear child. I will keep my part of the bargain. Presently, he will be as good as new."

"How could you do that to him? How could you do a thing like that?" Vanessa was shaking. She tried to stop herself, but she could not.

Professor Raeder observed her calmly. "Rage. Anger. Frustration. You would like me to die horribly before your very eyes... All perfectly natural. All perfectly natural. I do not blame you... But try — at least try — to see it from my point of view, Vanessa. I am about to rid this country of a tyrant — a despicable tyrant who will stop at nothing to achieve his ends. He ordered your death, Vanessa. Do not forget that."

"A tyrant — a despicable tyrant," she echoed, meeting Professor Raeder's gaze. "You give a very accurate description."

He smiled. "I take your point. There is an old adage about fighting fire with fire, is there not? The difference between Humboldt and myself is that I do not like the methods I am forced to use: he does ... Now, sit down, child. I realise it is late and you must rest. But there are matters we have to discuss. You must understand clearly what I require of you. Soon your ordeal will be over, and you and Dr. Badel will be free to do whatever you wish. It was necessary to stage this little demonstration to convince you that you should co-operate fully with me. In later years, doubtless, you will be glad that you did."

"In later years," said Vanessa, "I shall hate myself."

"So. That is your privilege. But now let us attend to the present. You are a unique paranormal, Vanessa. I have studied your records and I have discovered that you have the greatest receptivity quotient ever tested — at least, in this country. You can receive the telergetic insertions of several paranormals simultaneously. You can handle the imput, store it, and release it as required. I have access to the case history Dr. Lindemann has written. His experiments were crude, but the results are phenomenal."

"I did only what Dr. Lindemann asked me to do," said Vanessa. "I don't know anything about telergetic insertions or receptivity quotients."

"Dear child, there is no reason why you should. Leave all the theorising to me. Sufficient to say that tomorrow evening, with your help, I shall destroy Sir Joseph Humboldt. You will be the transmitter of the impulse, that is all."

"Why do you need me?" cried Vanessa. "Why must I be involved? Why can't you kill the Prime Minister like — like you killed Roland?"

Professor Raeder sighed. "My dear, Dr. Badel was in the immediate proximity of my little team. He was unprotected, he was in a stress situation, he was

163

psychologically vulnerable, he was open to suggestion. He was a sitting duck ... Some decades ago, in certain African tribes, the witch-doctor — a man respected and feared by the community — could command someone to die. The command would be carried out — not because the witch-doctor was all-powerful but because the victim believed him to be all-powerful. Such, roughly, was the case with Dr. Badel. He was a student when I was at the height of my professional career. He knows my work and he knows that I am one of the greatest living paranormal psychologists. Apart from Dimitrov in Russia and Dr. Sun in China, I am probably the best ... He was already subconsciously conditioned to accept my authority. He believed that I could kill him because he knew that I believed I could kill him. I might even have managed it without the assistance of our young friends. An interesting thought ... The acceptance by the educated mind of the witch-doctor motif. I might write a monograph upon it ... Still, I digress. You ask why I need you. I will tell you why. Or I will try to tell you why ... Do you know anything about gravity, or electro-magnetic radiation or the law of inverse squares?"

"Professor Raeder, I am seventeen years old and for most of my life I have been nothing but a guinea pig for people like Dr. Lindemann."

"I see. Lametable. But surely you understand the term telergy?"

"It is telepathic energy, I think."

"Yes, it is telepathic energy. A most mysterious entity. Like gravity, its source can be discovered and its effects defined and measured. But one cannot treat a beam of telergy like, for example, a beam of light, and measure its intensity and wave-length. On the other hand, one can focus telergy just as one can use a lens to focus

164

light ... Now, let us consider the analogue of light for a moment. Imagine the headlamp of an ordinary hover-car on a misty night. You can see the beam defined in the mist. What shape is it?"

"Like a great bar," said Vanessa.

"No, child," snapped Professor Raeder testily. "It is not like a great bar. Your imagination serves you ill. It is an extended cone. The apex is the source of light, the filament in the lamp, and the diameter of the base of the cone increases in proportion to its distance from the apex. Thus the intensity of the light delivered to the base varies inversely to the distance from the light emitted at source. Do I make myself clear?"

"No. I can't understand you."

Professor Raeder gave a deep sigh. "Good grief! We are raising a generation of illiterates ... No matter ... Let us try again. Let us take a different approach. We will stay with the analogue of light. Suppose I had a powerful searchlight, and suppose on a very clear night, I shone it upon an aircraft high in the sky. Would the beam of light that hit the aircraft be the same width as the beam emitted at source?"

Vanessa thought for a moment. "No. It would be broader."

"Precisely, And therefore less intense. But suppose I used a laser beam — a beam of coherent light?"

"It would retain its intensity," said Vanessa, suddenly perceiving what Professor Raeder was getting at.

"Precisely. Now, in telergetic terms, you have the capacity of changing a conventional beamed trans-mission into a coherent beamed transmission. In short, Vanessa, if telergy is channelled through you, you will be even better than a lens. You will transform it into a kind of telepathic laser beam ... Sir Joseph Humboldt, unlike Dr. Badel, is far from us in physical terms.

Moreover, he is protected by a highly trained group of paranormals who could easily block any weak transmissions. But they will not be able to block a telepathic laser. So, tomorrow evening, we will take Sir Joseph when he least expects it. Tomorrow, I happen to know that, after the dinner he is giving for the Israeli Prime Minister, he will leave Number Ten and spend the night with his mistress. She has a very discreet flat in Belgravia. The dogs will be there, of course. But Sir Joseph will be relaxed. And that is when we will strike."

"And afterwards? When Sir Joseph is dead?"

Professor Raeder smiled. "Let us think about that when Sir Joseph *is* dead, my dear. Now run along and get some sleep. Tomorrow, you will be given a simple conditioning technique. Then we shall be ready."

23

JENNY PARGETTER WOKE up screaming. Simon switched on the light.

"What is it love? What's happening? Did you have a nightmare?"

"Yes, I had a nightmare."

"Tell me about it."

"Vanessa. She is in the hands of a madman. He is called Reader or Raeder. Something like that. He has a collection of terrifying children — not his. Children who have escaped from schools for paranormals. It's in Scotland, I think."

"Raeder," mused Simon. "The name strikes a bell. There was a scandal some time ago . . . A parapsychologist . . . I think he had been doing naughty things with naughty little boys. Something like that . . . Raeder . . . Yes that was it. Professor Marius Raeder."

Jenny gave a deep sigh. "He's got Vanessa in Scotland. She doesn't know where, so I don't know where . . . This Raeder — he intends to use her to assassinate Black Joe." Jenny held her head in her hands. "Don't ask me how. I don't know how. I only pick up echoes from this child I rejected . . . Simon, we must call the police, or security, or whatever."

He looked at her searchingly. "Must we? Why? I thought you didn't care too much for Black Joe. He is the one who gave orders for Vanessa to be taken out. So it would be poetic justice if he gets taken out instead."

Jenny put her hands over her eyes. "Oh, God, I need a drink."

"Hot milk?"

"Don't be bloody silly . . . I'm sorry, darling. Brandy, whisky, vodka — any damn rotgut. Bring the bottle."

When Simon returned with a bottle of brandy and glasses, he tried to lighten the mood. "How about an orgy? Having an orgy with one's own wife could be rather trendy." It was the wrong thing to say.

Jenny withered him with a look. "We have to call the police — or security or whoever. It's obvious."

Simon handed her a very large brandy and poured one for himself. "Why is it obvious?"

"Because if Black Joe is killed — and, my God, I wish he'd drop dead from natural and painful causes — it is a stone cold certainty that this Raeder person will be able to pin the blame entirely on Vanessa. Then she will be in a worse fix than ever."

"She couldn't be," Simon pointed out. "Officially, she doesn't exist and unofficially she has to be killed anyway." He sipped his brandy and was silent for a few moments. Then he went on: "If Humboldt is killed, the present government will fall. If a general election were held, it's odds on that Tom Green would come out of it laughing. Can you imagine him giving orders to have Vanessa taken out? More likely she'd get the King's Pardon, a nominal sentence, and a life peerage within five years." He laughed. "That would be bloody marvellous, wouldn't it? Your little long-lost daughter changing the course of history."

Jenny swallowed her brandy and sat in bed, thinking. "This man Raeder is probably right round the twist," she said at length. "But people like that are very cunning. Suppose his plan — whatever it is — succeeds. He might then fix it so that Vanessa takes the entire blame, with him coming out of it looking whiter than white. Alternatively, having used her, he might just kill her. As you pointed out, she does not now officially exist. So how could he get smashed for killing a non-existent girl? No, Simon, much as I would like to see Joe Humboldt dead, we must call the police. It's Vanessa's only hope. If they can find her in time, this man Raeder can be made to talk, and her innocence will be established." She held out her glass for more brandy. "Even a wretch like Humboldt ought to be grateful for having his life saved."

Simon poured more brandy for Jenny and for himself. "Come back to reality, sweetheart. If we call the police or security now, they just might conceivably trace Vanessa before this crackpot Raeder can put his plans — whatever they are — into operation. In which case, they will quietly eliminate both of them. You must know that as well as I do. But if they don't find Vanessa until after the deed is done, the result will still be the same. It will take time for Tom Green to gain power and assume authority over the security forces. By the time he is in a position to establish her existence, commend her innocence, etcetera, she will be dead. I do not think posthumous recognition will mean much to her or to you. So, let us not call the police."

"I am going to." Jenny gazed at him, white-faced. "It's her only chance."

"No, love, you are not." For once, Simon was adamant. "Because if you do, you and I are both dead. Officially, Vanessa does not exist. If we now claim that she does, Humboldt's boys will probe us again for information then silence us." He gave a grim laugh. "Or do you think they will give us a vote of thanks for being co-operative?"

"I already loathe myself so much I'm not even sure I want to live," moaned Jenny. "And you are saying that I have to abandon her yet again."

"It's the only way to give her a chance."

"I must do something!"

"Right. We will do something," said Simon. "We'll take the hovercar to Scotland and go looking for her."

"But I don't know where she is ... I can't even be absolutely sure it is Scotland."

"You might get more information from her en route — particularly if you try to doze or keep your mind open ... I know it's a lousy gamble, darling. But it is all I can suggest. At least it is something to do."

"Yes," echoed Jenny, "at least it is something to do."

Sir Joseph Humboldt had had a liaison with Maria Mancini for several years. Signora Mancini was the widow of an Italian ambassador who had died in a plane crash shortly after Sir Joseph had begun to take an interest in his wife.

The liaison was an open secret in political and diplomatic circles — the kind of open secret that, in Britain, was whispered about rather than talked about. A gutter-press journalist who had linked their names together in his column less for political idealism than for personal advancement apparently committed suicide three days later. A tri-di anchor man who made some unfortunate allusion during a programme on the Prime Minister's career went berserk one evening in Oxford Street and was later committed to an asylum for the criminally insane.

Although over the years Sir Joseph had taken and continued to take — despite his advanced years — much pleasure in the sensual delights afforded by Maria Mancini's well-endowed and extremely Italian body, he had never felt the slightest inclination to marry her. It would have been politically undesirable. Sir Joseph was by no means handsome, but he knew that he was physically impressive. He had been compared by various political commentators with Lloyd George in his prime. Lloyd George could never have been described as handsome; but he had certainly been magnetic. Sir Joseph knew that he, also, had a similar effect — particularly upon the predatory middle-aged women who, if not the backbone of his party, were certainly its mailed fist. A fat Italian wife, however delightful between the sheets, would have cost him at least a million votes. It was too high a price to pay for pneumatic bliss.

But though Sir Joseph was unwilling to give Signora Mancini the marriage she desperately craved, he had managed to provide her with compensations. She was received at Court, she dined at the best houses, she had unlimited credit and an extraordinary collection of jewellery, and she could use aspiring junior ministers as errand boys. It was something to be seen with the royals at Ascot. It was something to be consulted by the Italian premier about Britain's policy towards the Middle East oil countries. She was wise enough not to demand too much.

As Sir Joseph called Signora Mancini on the scrambled V-phone in his bedroom, he was wondering not how to counter the Israeli Prime Minister's protest at Britain's failure to deliver five nuclear strike submarines because of pressure from the oil-bearing Arab states, but how to cope with a recent and inexplicable loss of sexual potency.

Maria Mancini's face came on the screen. "Darleeng,"

she said. "How sweet of you to call. I was not expecting it because of thees Israeli business. Is eet a dreadful bore?"

Sir Joseph, as always, was entranced by her accent and her insistence on using British slang that had died with Somerset Maugham.

"It is a dreadful bore, my love. Quite tiresome." He found himself slipping emphatically into the same kind of idiom. "I shall probably have to concede two submarines by the end of this year, and three by the end of next. Secretly, of course. In public, Mr. Mendelson will scream about betrayal, and in public I shall utter wisely on the balance of power . . . The dinner should be over by ten, my sweet. I will give instructions that it must be over by ten. Therefore I should be with you by ten-thirty."

Signora Mancini registered the information about the submarines for transmission to Rome. It might be good for a million new lire. Then she recalled her role as alluring mistress, and made sure that the V-lens caught her bosom. The dress she wore was décolleté — about as décolleté as you could get.

"Will you wish to eat?" she enquired.

"My love," responded Sir Joseph gallantly, "I will wish to eat you."

"No. Stupid of me. You will not wish to eat," she pouted. "However, you may like a spoonful of caviar, perhaps, to be washed down with Veuve Clicquot."

"My dear, I shall eat you."

She laughed, a full-throated Italian laugh. "I still have bruises from your last meal."

Sir Joseph Humboldt picked up his cue, found his exit line. "Unto them that hath shall be given," he quoted. Then he cut the connection just in case Maria did not understand and required an explanation.

24

THERE SEEMED TO be unending fog in Roland Badel's mind. He could not think very clearly, he could not remember things, he felt desperately tired. Some time ago, a youth — Alfred? — had brought him something to eat and drink. Was it meant to be breakfast or lunch? He didn't know. Perhaps it was not important. After he had eaten, he had felt more sleepy than ever. He had been thankful just to lie down on his bed and relax. He had an idea that Vanessa had visited him, accompanied by that maniac Raeder. But it could have been a dream. Only a dream.

Groping desperately through the fog, Roland tried to pull himself together. The food or the drink had obviously been drugged. That would be the paranoid professor's style.

The paranoid professor . . .

He giggled foolishly.

There once was a paranoid professor
whose mistress wouldn't let him carress her . . .

No! Stop that! Think!

He thought. He thought about Vanessa . . .

There once was a paranoid professor
who wanted a girl named Vanessa . . .

No! No! No! Think!

He slapped his own face savagely in the hope that the

173

pain would penetrate his mind, clear his wits. He was weak, and he couldn't hurt himself enough.

There once was ... *No!*

He had an inspiration. He bit his finger. There seemed to be quite a lot of strength left in his jaws. He bit his finger till the pain seemed to come like an arrow of light through the mental fog. He bit his finger until he wanted to cry out. He bit his finger until he began to cough and splutter as a strange fluid poured down his throat.

After a time he knew what it was. Blood.

That connected. He lay on the bed, weak, sweating, with a finger throbbing where it had been bitten through to the bone. But the fog was lifting. It was like surfacing after a drinking jag. Surfacing the hard way.

He must remember not to eat anything more, not to drink anything more. He would be no good to Vanessa if he were in a perpetual stupor. He would have to get his mind clear and then try to do something. Death or glory.

He laughed weakly.

Death, he had already tried.

The door opened. Enter the paranoid professor. Roland tried to sit up, and fell back.

"Good evening, Dr. Badel ... Dear me, we are in a mess, aren't we? Blood everywhere. What have you been doing, my dear fellow? Ah, biting your fingers, I see. What a curious diversion. We shall have to clean you up. We shall have to get you sensible, also."

"I am already sensible," said Roland thickly.

Raeder laughed. "A subjective opinion rather than a professional one. I will return in a few minutes with bandages. It looks as if your finger may need a couple of stitches. You really should not be quite so perverse."

Roland fainted while his finger was being stitched. He was not out long. He returned to consciousness in time to see a hypodermic needle being withdrawn from his arm.

"So. You are with us once more. Do not try to move for a while. I have given you a stimulant. Let it do its work. You are shortly going to witness the generation of long-range telergetic euthanasia, Dr. Badel. You should find it very interesting. You will need a clear mind to observe carefully. After all, there is your future to think of."

"My future?" said Roland grimly. He wanted to ask what had just been pumped into him, but decided against it. There was little point. Whatever Raeder said, he would not be inclined to believe it. Nevertheless, he was beginning to feel stronger, his mind was becoming clearer. Perhaps it was just an ordinary stimulant, or something to neutralise the drug that was in his system. "I have no illusions about my future, Professor Raeder. Nor, I am happy to say, does yours seem particularly bright."

The Professor remained jovial. "Dear boy, away with pessimism and depressive thoughts. In time to come, you will see that I have acted for the best — for you, for Vanessa. Dammit, for the entire nation. When the present tyranny has been removed, there will be room for men like you. That I promise."

"Professor Raeder, if you promised me that the sun would rise tomorrow, I should doubt the phenomenon for the first time."

"Splendid. I see you have recovered yourself. Now, if you feel up to it, we will join our little group of gifted youngsters ... A warning — unnecessary, I am sure. Do not interfere with the experiment. I should hate to burn a hole in your brain after having meticulously repaired the damage you have done to your finger. Such a waste! Also, please, do not, please,

175

attempt to speak to Vanessa. She is in a very vulnerable and relaxed state. I have spent most of the day implanting a simple but necessary conditioned reflex in her. If you attempt to interfere with the sequences of my programme, I cannot answer for her sanity or, indeed, her life."

25

THE ROOM WAS darkened. Vanessa lay on her back, motionless, on a trolly. A beam of red light from a lamp standard close to the trolly focussed on her open eyes. In the semi-darkness, Roland could see the members of Professor Raeder's group of paranormals dotted about the room, sitting in relaxed positions in comfortable chairs. Their eyes were open, but none of them moved.

"Sub-threshold hypnosis," said Professor Raeder. "I trust you are impressed. It has taken time to establish, of course. I have a system of key-words. Using the key-words in post-hypnotic suggestion, I can cause the patient to enter a condition of sub-threshold hypnosis upon command. But, as distinct from full hypnosis, sub-threshold hypnosis does not inhibit paranormal talent. In fact, the patient retains every faculty except independence of will. The others were already conditioned, and their conditioning was established over a period of time. It is unfortunate that I had to use a crash-programme on Vanessa. It has been rather tiring. However the results are quite rewarding. Her mind is now completely open, Dr. Badel. She will accept, contain and, upon command, discharge under guidance the energy deposited by our young friends... It is now shortly after midnight. I expect Sir Joseph will be feeling quite relaxed. We do not have long to wait. Please be seated in that chair." He indicated a chair in a corner of the room. "And kindly do not move from it. Under no circumstances should you move from it unless you have my authority."

Roland did not move. He was looking intently at Vanessa. Her eyes seemed vacant, and yet . . . And yet, somehow, he sensed that the vacancy was not entirely convincing.

"Please, Dr. Badel." Professor Raeder motioned with his laser pistol. "No one would notice if I were compelled to kill you now. The project would still continue. Be a good fellow and relax in your chair. Vanessa has already endured much for your sake. Do not de-value her sacrifice. You are a trained scientist. Observe and remember. That is all."

Roland looked at the laser pistol, and shrugged. "You are right, Professor Raeder. I am a trained scientist. I will observe and remember." He took himself groggily to the chair indicated and sank down on to it. There was sweat on his forehead, and his knees felt absurdly weak. He would have liked to believe that what he was experiencing was simply a nightmare. But he knew that it was a dreadful reality.

Professor Raeder remained standing, still watching Roland cautiously, still pointing the laser pistol at him.

"London!" he said in a loud voice, apparently to no one in particular. "Seek target."

There was a silence, stretching into minutes, then:

"Target found." It was Janine's voice. "Target found . . . In bed . . . Woman . . . Oh, it's lovely! . . . Oh, lost! Blocks! Blocks!"

"Glasgow!" called Professor Raeder. "Neutralise

blocks. Reassure. Neautralise blocks and give re-assurance."

Again silence. Then Alfred's voice. "Blocks neutralised. Reassurance ... Blocks not with target ... Blocks tired, relaxing, close but not very close ... Believe now target enjoying himself ..."

"Target found again. Woman ... Lovely! Lovely!" Locked into target .. Locked into woman ... Lovely!" shrieked Janine.

"London, Glasgow, hold," called Professor Raeder. "Paris, Berlin, stand by to enter London ... Enter ..."

"London entered." It was Robert's voice.

"Suggest completion, satisfaction to target."

"London entered." Sandra's voice.

"Compel target's rejection of woman."

Roland watched and listened fascinated. Watched and listened while Professor Raeder's laser pistol pointed at him unwaveringly. Here was history being made — a dreadful kind of history.

"Oh! Oh! It's over. It's stopped." Janine's voice was full of disappointment. "They pull apart."

"Satisfaction suggested."

"Rejection achieved."

"London, Glasgow, Paris, Berlin hold. Come in Warsaw. Enter London. What do you find?"

"Target and woman apart now." It was the voice of Quasimodo. "Target puzzled. Target puzzled but not afraid."

"All hold!" Professor Raeder's voice was hard but calm. "All hold! Glasgow maintain neutralisation of blocks. Remain detached ... Others maintain unity. Hold target. Maintain unity. Increase power now. Maximum hold ... Prepare to transfer."

Roland, still painfully conscious of the laser pistol in

Professor Raeder's steady hand, peered through the semi-darkness. The young paranormals were no longer relaxed. Their eyes had closed. They moved restlessly in their chairs, groaning, grunting. Janine let out a high-pitched giggle. Quasimodo made a noise that sounded almost like an animal snarl. Sandra whimpered.

"We are ready." Again it was Quasimodo. "Power is good. Target held. We are ready."

"Athens is open," said the Professor. "Athens is open and waiting. Seek total unity. *Transfer to Athens!*" The final command was a shout.

On her trolly, Vanessa twitched, shivered, shook. She let out a great cry of anguish. Then her body became limp once more, though her eyes remained open.

"London, have you found unity?"

Vanessa's lips moved, but it was Janine's voice that spoke. "We have found unity."

"Paris, have you found unity?"

Again Vanessa's lips moved; but it was Robert's voice. "We have found unity."

"Berlin, have you found unity?"

Now Vanessa's lips and Sandra's voice. "We have found unity."

Roland watched, fascinated, horrified. The techniques devised by Professor Raeder were brilliant and terrible.

"Warsaw, have you found unity?" The Professor's voice remained extraordinarily calm.

"We have found unity."

"Have you become one?"

Vanessa answered — impossibly in a chorus of five voices. "We have become one."

"Athens will hold you. Now, all of you are Athens only. The target is held by Athens. I will count ten. Hold your power, let it grow. I will count ten. Then I will command. One, two, three, four, five, six, seven, eight, nine, ten . . . *Strike!* "

In a room directly below the bedroom occupied by Sir Joseph Humboldt and Maria Mancini, the three night paras — one woman and two men — played cards.

The woman stiffened, froze. "I sense something." She closed her eyes.

The two men also closed their eyes, concentrating. Presently they opened their eyes. One poured another glass of non-alcoholic wine.

"I found nothing."

"Nor did I . . . Shit, I hate this night duty, and I hate this non-alcoholic gnat-piss."

"Did you go in deep?"

"Think I'm a fool? Joe doesn't like voyeurs when he's banging away. If he felt a deep probe, he'd put us all on the bread line. State bloody secrets are all he's afraid of losing. And he's not thinking about them when he's lying on top of the Italian cow."

The woman still had her eyes closed. "I sense something."

One of the men yawned. "Knock it off, sweetie. You're probably getting reflections from Maria. Joe must have a hard on by now. He's probably slipping it to her at this very moment; and because you are a woman you are getting peripheral transmission."

She was obstinate. "I still sense something."

"Forget it. How many hours of duty have you put in this week?"

"Maybe sixty."

"Then you are over the top, love. Forget about Joe. Come back to us. If anybody tries to flash him, we'll all feel it . . . Whose deal?"

The woman opened her eyes and yawned. "God. I

hate night duty ... For the record, since you have seniority, Jack, I interpret that as an order. Incidentally, it's my deal. Goodness, I seem to be winning a lot."

Sir Joseph Humboldt rolled away from Maria Mancini. Something was wrong. He knew he had not achieved orgasm, and yet he felt as if he had. It had happened before — he was no longer able to perform like a young stud — but not with this feeling of having attained satisfaction when he knew that he had not.

He hoped Maria had not noticed his inadequacy. Probably she hadn't. Usually, she managed to have three or four herself even before he got the show on the road.

"Joseph, my dearest, what ees it? Tell naughty little Maria what ees wrong? Am I too greedy? I hunger for you so."

He was glad of the darkness. He didn't want to see her face. He stretched out a hand to stroke and squeeze her ample breast. Sometimes even the merest touch of her breast would be enough to renew his ardour. But tonight it wasn't. Tonight her breast felt only like warm meat; soft, flabby meat. He took his hand away, disappointed. He knew that she felt his disappointment.

"What ees it, Joseph, man of mine? Shall I switch on the light? You are tired?"

"No, don't touch the light. I am all right, thank you." How he hated that theatrical phrase 'man of mine'. It was Maria's favourite endearment. Silly Italian cow!

"Something ees wrong," she persisted. "I did not please you."

"Nothing is wrong, Maria. You did please me. Stop fretting." He tried to make his voice sound gentle, and failed. There was a sound of muffled sobbing. Maria was crying into her pillow. Blast the woman!

182

Something was wrong. He shivered, feeling cold, but not physically cold. It couldn't be a probe. The duty paras would block it. But something was wrong. He wanted to be alone. He didn't know why he wanted to be alone. Normally, by this time, he would be counting the bruises on that soft Italian flesh and spilling champagne over those voluptuous breasts as Maria indulged her customary appetite for the after-play of love.

"Leave me. Go to your own room. Get a drink or something. I want to be alone." He heard his own voice. He didn't believe it. It sounded so impersonal. Something was wrong.

"I will switch on the — "

"Leave the bloody light!" he roared. "And leave me!" He wanted to say he was sorry, but the words stuck in his throat. Something *was* wrong.

Wordlessly, Maria got out of bed. He thought he could see her in the darkness, but he could not. She stumbled, then found the bedroom door and opened it. A shaft of light displayed her body in cruel silhouette. Fat, shapeless Italian cow! He marvelled that he had put up with her so long. Full belly, sagging breasts. You could find better in any decent brothel. Then the door closed, and he was in darkness once more.

He breathed a sigh of relief. But, still, something was wrong.

Something was indeed wrong.

But by then it was too late.

The darkness glowed.

He stared at the glow incredulously. He wanted to cry out. He opened his mouth to call for the paras. But no sound came.

He stared hypnotised. The glow assumed outline, contours. It became the incandescent shape of a girl.

"My name is Vanessa," said the girl. "You ordered my death." She glowed pulsatingly, blindingly.

"No! No!" Sir Joseph Humboldt did not know whether his protest was vocal or if he were only shrieking in his mind.

"My name is Vanessa Smith," went on the girl relentlessly. "You tried to destroy me, and now I will destroy you."

"No! Please, please, no! I have so much to do. You don't realise. There is so much responsibility!" He knew now that the words did not issue from his mouth. His mouth had been silenced. The words could only form in his mind.

The phantasm advanced. "I will lie with you, Sir Joseph Humboldt. I am fire, you are flesh. I will lie with you. My kiss shall burn the flesh from your jaw, my embrace shall consume your manhood, my arms, caressing you, will expose the charred ribs. Truly, it will be a great consummation."

"*No!*"

She came towards him, glowing, pulsating, burning. He could feel the heat. Somehow, he managed to get out of bed. He was naked and felt naked. He knew now that there could be no more defence, but life was precious. So precious.

He backed away towards the window. She followed him. He felt the heat. Rationality had sped. He was in no condition to consider the philosophical implications of an apparent woman of fire. He backed away. The phantasm followed.

Somehow he managed to open the french windows. The air outside was clean, cool, moist. Perhaps it would help him to drive back this apparition.

He half-walked, half-fell on to the small balcony. The hour was late, Belgravia was quiet. He wanted to call

184

upon the citizens of London to rise to his defence. But, in a moment of clarity, he knew that none would wish to defend him. He knew, at last, that he was alone.

The phantasm was inexorable. "One kiss only, my dear Sir Joseph. A kiss before dying."

"No! No!" He recoiled in horror.

He leaned backwards. The phantasm advanced.

He leaned backwards, and fell with a long despairing cry.

The phantasm dissolved.

The paras in the room below heard Sir Joseph's cry. Signora Maria Mancini heard his cry.

But there was nothing to be done.

Vanessa sighed.

Professor Raeder said: "Welcome home, Athens. It is accomplished?"

"It is accomplished." The voice was Quasimodo's.

"Rest easy, then, Athens. I am well pleased. At the count of ten, you will execute my command. One, two, three, four, five, six, seven, eight, nine, ten. *Disperse*!"

Suddenly, the inert paranormals in the room began to stir, to shake themselves, rub their eyes.

Only Vanessa remained motionless.

Professor Raeder gazed at her. "So. Athens, perhaps, remains in shock. I will test her E.E.G. recording."

Alfred was the first to recover full consciousness.

"Alfred, dear boy, I congratulate you for your efficient block. Kindly hold this laser pistol and point it meaningfully at Dr. Badel while I investigate Vanessa's condition. Soon we shall all rest, but one wishes to leave matters tidy."

Alfred, still yawning, took the laser pistol and held it towards Roland. Professor Raeder wheeled what was

185

apparently an electro-encephalogram machine towards Vanessa's trolly, and placed the helmet on her head.

"Amazing! She is still supercharged. Theoretically it is not possible. All the energy should have been discharged at Sir Joseph Humboldt. But she is still supercharged. How can this be?"

The others, Janine, Quasimodo and the rest, were showing signs of life.

Roland Badel thought it was now or never. He had a flash of inspiration.

"Throw it back at them, Vanessa!" he shouted. "Throw it all back at them! Athens, reject"

Vanessa groaned.

Professor Raeder glanced at Alfred. "Kill him, boy. He has presumed."

But Alfred's eyes opened wide. He shuddered and fell backwards, contorting, gibbering.

Professor Raeder scrambled for the laser pistol. He got it. Even in the semi-darkness, Roland Badel could see his smile of triumph.

Suddenly, the laser pistol fell from Raeder's hand. He looked down in amazement. Then he dropped on all fours and began to bark like a dog. Then he gobbled like a turkey. Then he fell foaming at the mouth, twitched a little and lay still.

Quasimodo stood up. He looked at Roland. Without a word he fell on his face. Janine stirred, suddenly contorted into the womb position, moaned pitiously and lay still.

Robert and Sandra barely moved. They whispered and died.

There was silence in the darkened room.

Unsteadily, Roland Badel rose to his feet. He staggered across to the trolly on which Vanessa lay.

"Vanessa, my darling love, how are you?"

She looked at him. She looked at him with eyes wide with innocence. She looked at him with the anxious, wondering gaze of a child.

"Daddy? You are my daddy, aren't you? You have come to take me home."

Clinically, Dr. Roland Badel observed the symptoms of withdrawal. "Yes, I have come to take you home."

"You are my daddy?"

His heart broke. Except that hearts do not break. He wanted to die. He wanted to live. He looked at the pale, beautiful girl who had regressed to childhood.

"Yes, Vanessa, I am your daddy."

"And you love me?"

"I love you."

"I have had nightmares. Terrible nightmares. Please take me home ... Have I been a good girl?"

It was such an innocent question. "Yes, Vanessa, you have been a very good girl, and I will take you home."

"And I will stay with you for ever?"

"Yes, you will stay with me for ever."

Vanessa sat up. "I had a bad dream," she said. "But I suppose all little girls have bad dreams ... They do, don't they?"

"Yes, my dear. All little girls have bad dreams."

"Is it morning?"

"I don't know. Let's find out."

Roland went to the window and flung back the curtains. "Yes, it is almost morning."

There was a grey light in the sky. Soon the sun would climb. Vanessa got off the trolly, gazed at the dead around her.

"Who are all these people, Daddy? Why are they sleeping on the floor?"

"They were very tired, Vanessa. They did not have time to go to bed."

"Can we go home now? I don't want to stay here. Something feels wrong."

"Yes, my dear. We can go home."

Somehow, Roland managed to get her out of the house. He remembered Professor Raeder's warnings about the mines. He didn't care a damn. In the half-light he took Vanessa away from the house, expecting death at any moment. It would have been welcome.

But death did not come. Either the proximity mines had been de-activated or he and Vanessa were just plain lucky. Either way, it did not matter.

"How far is home, Daddy?"

"A long way, Vanessa. We may have to cross an ocean. Will you mind?"

She held his hand tightly. "Not if I am with you."

CODA

With the sensational death of Sir Joseph Humboldt, the government fell. The British Unity Party, an authoritarian political force spawned by the all-party Law-and-Order movement in the turbulent 1970s, was helpless without its acknowledged leader, thus displaying the inherent weakness of monolithic political systems.

In the general election which followed, the New Consensus Party — radical-liberal in its basic attitudes — gained an overwhelming victory. Upon becoming Prime Minister, the Right Honourable Thomas Green, M.P., dismissed the Security of the State Bill which his predecessor had hoped to translate into an Act of Parliament. Later, he was largely responsible for the existence of an international treaty, under the aegis of the United Nations, which banned the development of paranormal talent for any purposes other than psychotherapy, strictly controlled scientific and medical research, and space communications.

At the precise moment of Sir Joseph Humboldt's death, Jenny Pargetter was dozing in the hovercar which her husband was driving towards the Scottish Highlands. She woke up and screamed. Simon's attention was distracted. The hovercar crashed head-on with a heavy transit vehicle. Simon Pargetter was killed instantly. Jenny, with both legs amputated above the knee, survived her injuries. But she took her own life after reading the account of her daughter's experience which was published in the major newspapers of the world and which was partly responsible for inspiring Britain to take the case of the international exploitation of paranormal children to the United Nations.

Dr. John Lindemann managed to flee to the U.S.S.R., where his skilled services were gratefully accepted — until the account of Vanessa Smith's ordeal was made public. At which time, he disappeared, his fate being unknown. British and U.S. intelligence assumed that he had been liquidated as a source of political embarrassment.

Professor Holroyd, Principal of Random Hill Residential School, died apparently by his own hand a few hours before the death of Sir Joseph Humboldt. At the inquest, experts in calligraphy refused to testify that the suicide note was genuine. A verdict of murder, by a person or persons unknown, was given.

Richard Haynes, First Private Secretary to Sir Joseph Humboldt, became an alcoholic. After learning the true account of Vanessa Smith's experiences, he voluntarily entered a psychiatric hospital. On being pronounced cured, he asked to remain at the hospital, working there for many years as a porter.

Maria Mancini returned to Italy and married a man considerably younger than herself, an ambitious member of the Diplomatic Service. She never returned to the United Kingdom.

Dr. Roland Badel, under the name of Oliver Anderson, eventually took Vanessa Smith, believing herself to be his daughter, to San Francisco, where he rapidly established himself as an artist of some importance. The account of Vanessa's experiences that he sent to the news media contained enough detail to establish

thenticity, but gave no reference to her whereabouts.
All the letters bore a Peruvian post-mark.

Vanessa Smith died at the age of thirty-two of
advanced physical senility. But even to the end, she
retained the mind and spirit of a small child. She died
with a teddy-bear called Dugal in her arms.

Upon her death, her body was cremated and the
ashes flown back to England to be buried by the side
of a casket containing the ashes of a child called Dugal
Nemo.

Oliver Anderson, naturalised American, survived her
by thirteen years. His most well-known painting — a
portrait entitled *Prisoner of Fire* — for which in his
lifetime he refused all offers, was sold for one hundred
and eighty thousand dollars after his death.

An unknown person established a fund whereby one
white rose and one red were to be placed daily upon the
graves of Vanessa Smith and Dugal Nemo in perpetuity.

SCIENCE FICTION FROM CORONET

EDMUND COOPER

☐	16464 6	Transit	30p
☐	21242 X	Prisoner Of Fire	60p
☐	10904 1	Five To Twelve	35p
☐	15132 3	The Uncertain Midnight	40p
☐	15091 2	The Last Continent	40p
☐	19478 2	The Cloud Walker	35p
☐	16216 1	Kronk	35p

POUL ANDERSON

☐	16337 2	Beyond The Beyond	35p
☐	16336 4	Tau Zero	35p
☐	19864 8	Ensign Flandry	65p
☐	20753 1	Flandry Of Terra	70p

All these books are available at your local bookshop or newsagent, o can be ordered direct from the publisher. Just tick the titles you want and fill in the form below.

Prices and availability subject to change without notice.

CORONET BOOKS, P.O. Box 11, Falmouth, Cornwall.

Please send cheque or postal order, and allow the following for postage and packing:

U.K. — One book 19p plus 9p per copy for each additional book ordered, up to a maximum of 73p.

B.F.P.O. and EIRE — 19p for the first book plus 9p per copy for the next 6 books, thereafter 3p per book.

OTHER OVERSEAS CUSTOMERS — 20p for the first book and 10p per copy for each additional book.

Name...

Address..

....